BERRIED ALIVE

APPLE ORCHARD COZY MYSTERY BOOK 4

CHELSEA THOMAS

Big +
LiTTLe
PRESS

To the Cozy Crew

"Reading brings us unknown friends."
— Honoré de Balzac

1

HOW NOW, BROWN COW?

"Chelsea and Miss May! Get over here. I need you to solve a super mysterious coffee shop mystery!" Brian smiled at us from behind the counter at the *Brown Cow.*

I squinted at him through a fog of early morning grogginess. "Mystery? At this hour?"

Brian laughed. But I was serious. It was 7:56 AM on a Sunday. I was wearing sweatpants I had owned for twenty years. My blond hair was frizzy with a nest of tangles.

It was too early for me to be awake, let alone solving mysteries.

Miss May, on the other hand, was bright-eyed and mushy-tailed. *Is that the expression? Mushy? Bushy? Whatever.* She was wide awake. And her eyes flickered with anticipation as soon as Brian said the word 'mystery..'

She leaned toward Brian with a smirk. "You say something mysterious has occurred at your quaint, small-town coffee shop?"

Brian smiled and gave us the low-down on the crime.

Apparently, he had shown up about half an hour late for

work that morning. And when he'd gotten there, his cash register and counter had been covered in sticky notes.

"It was a mosaic of sticky yellow squares," he said in his SoCal drawl. "I think it was a prank pulled by one of my sneaky staff members. But I'm not sure whodunit."

Miss May gave Brian a playful grin. "Hmmm. I don't know. Not sure we want to help Boss-Man Brian punish a light-hearted prankster at work."

"You know I'm not going to do that, Miss May. I want to figure out who the jokester is so I can get them back with a prank of my own." Brian said. "And you two are expert mystery-solvers by now. So I need your help."

"The technical term for 'mystery-solvers' is 'sleuths,'" Miss May said.

"You know what I mean." Brian looked off into the distance. "I think for my revenge, I shall fill their shoes with slime."

I grunted. "I think your victim will suspect something is amiss as soon as you ask them to take off their shoes."

"Good point," Brian said. "I'll plot my revenge later. But I can't do anything if I don't know who did it. And I can't figure it out for the life of me."

Brian gestured behind me and Miss May. "Plus. All these people want to see the famous Pine Grove detectives at work! You're not going to disappoint your fans, are you?"

Miss May and I turned around. Indeed, an elderly couple, a young family and a few stragglers had gathered behind us.

"I think this crowd has gathered for coffee," Miss May said.

The elderly woman stepped forward. "You're wrong about that one, missy! I want to see you two genius sleuths at work." The old woman held up her phone. "Also can I get a pic with you gals?"

Miss May smiled. She and I had solved several mysteries together by that point, and the selfie request from the old woman was not our first. But our minor celebrity status still felt novel and surprisingly flattering.

"Of course," Miss May said.

The old woman handed her phone to her grouchy husband. Then she jumped between me and Miss May, smiled and held up a peace sign for the photo.

"OK," she said after reviewing the photo. "Great pic. Now. Solve the mystery!"

Miss May wavered but the crowd egged her on.

"Yeah!"

"Solve it!"

"Crack the case!"

Miss May held up her hands to quiet the onlookers. "OK. We'll take a look and see what we can do. Brian, can you bring your employees out here?"

Brian pumped his fist. "Nice. This is so fun. You and Chelsea are local treasures, you know."

"Just get them over here," Miss May said.

A few seconds later, Brian had lined up the two members of his staff in front of the counter to be questioned by Miss May.

First came Rita, an old high school classmate of mine. Rita and I had gone from frenemies to friends after I'd moved back to Pine Grove, and she had played a huge role in the first mystery Miss May and I had solved.

That day, Rita looked striking as always. Curly hair. Olive skin. Perfect smile. I wondered how she managed to look so good while raising a baby on her own, but that was a mystery for another day.

Brian's other employee was a girl in her early 20's known as Willow. I had no idea if Willow was her real name or not, but it was fitting. Willow was a genuine 21st-century hippie, with dreadlocks and a nose ring and a tattoo of every phase of the moon climbing gracefully up her forearm.

"Both these girls were here before I got in this morning," Brian said. "And neither will fess up to anything."

Rita and Willow looked at one another and smirked.

"I see," Miss May said. "Perhaps there is a bond of secrecy between them. What do you think, Chelsea? Any initial theories?"

Although Miss May had been hesitant to begin this 'investigation,' once she started, she was all in. That meant that I was all in with her.

"It's possible they worked together," I said.

"True," Miss May said. "Would you ladies do me a favor and empty your pockets?"

Another smirk between the employees. They both emptied their pockets onto the counter, but neither was carrying anything suspicious. Mostly spare change and lint. Plus a tube of cherry-flavored lip balm.

A balding man called out from the crowd, "This store has security cameras! What if you check those?"

Miss May shook her head. "That's cheating. And I don't think it's what Brian had in mind when he asked us to solve the mystery."

"You got that right," Brian said. "I want some genuine detective work."

"May we walk around the counter?" Miss May said.

Brian nodded and Miss May stalked behind the cash register. I followed like a loyal hound dog on the scent.

Once I got a look at the counter, I cracked up laughing. Almost half the work surface was still covered in sticky notes. And each sticky note had a little message written on it in messy handwriting.

I turned to Brian. "I thought you said you cleared off all the sticky notes!"

Brian chuckled in chagrin. "Yeah. That's just my personal collection. I guess I do kind of have a thing for convenient, sticky paper. That's why it was a good prank."

"That's not even as bad as it gets," Rita said. "Some days there's like three times as many."

Miss May squatted down and read a few of the notes out loud.

"Greet every customer as if they are your mom!"

"A smile goes a thousand miles!"

"Make each cup with genuine kindness!"

My aunt looked up, eyes twinkling. "No wonder the service in this place is so good, Brian."

"I hire good people," Brian said. "When they aren't playing tricks on me."

"I don't suspect your employees actually committed this crime," Miss May said. "Would you agree, Chelsea?"

No clue. Need coffee, I thought. But I managed to sputter out a few words. "Yup. Agree. Totally! The prankster is not Rita or Willow. Someone else sticky-noted this joint."

Miss May scratched her head. "Then tell us, Chels. Who could it have been?"

I glared at Miss May. She was having fun putting me on the spot, and she knew I didn't know the answer. But the crowd was waiting for me to speak, and I could feel my hands starting to clam up with stress.

I looked around the room to figure out who, other than the employees, could have played the practical joke. That's when I spotted a conspicuous table along the far wall.

There were only two cups on the table, but there were

seven or eight used tea bags on saucers beside the mugs. Whoever had been sitting at that table had been there for quite a while.

Perhaps, I reasoned, *he or she was already at the Brown Cow before Brian had arrived that morning.*

Miss May followed my line of sight over to the table and smirked. "What do you think, Chelsea? Could the suspect be one of Brian's customers, not an employee?"

An excited murmur erupted throughout the room. The patrons were thrilled by the prospect that one of their own could've perpetrated the practical joke. But the trill of excitement exacerbated my hand sweat. *Gross.*

"I do think it's possible," I said, wiping my hands on my jeans. "But which one of these fine people could it have been?"

Suddenly, an angry man stormed into the shop, pushed his way through the crowd, and slammed his fist down on the counter. "I want my coffee and I want it immediately and I want it now and I want it dark and I want it rich!"

I recognized the man as local rabble-rouser Wallace the Traveler. Wallace was bald. And paunchy. He wore the same pair of stained, oversized khakis every day. And he also wore a light blue sweater with a large hole in the back. The look was topped off with a pair of bifocals that Wallace wore down on his nose. And he never left home without a personality so gruff, it could shock a lightbulb out of its socket.

Pine Grove did not have a lot of strangers like Wallace roaming the streets, and his recent emergence in our small town was one of the biggest mysteries of the prior months. Neither Miss May nor I had tried to solve that particular quandary. We agreed that Wallace's life was none of our business.

But questions swirled about town, nonetheless. Many suspected Wallace was homeless. Others thought he might take the bus up from the city every day for the fresh country air. No one knew for sure, but everyone seemed to have had their own uncomfortable "Wallace experience." *Including me.*

One day, when I was running errands in town, Wallace had followed me across the street singing "Mary Had a Little Lamb" at the top of his lungs. I'd tried to keep my head down and continue walking, but Wallace had jumped in front of me and screamed, "I'm the lamb! Look at me. I am the lamb!"

It had been a chilling moment. *And I love lambs.*

So... yeah. Wallace's presence in the coffee shop that morning transformed my trickle of palm sweat into a flash flood. Fortunately, Brian was far more relaxed about his unruly customer.

"Hey man, we're kind of in the middle of something here," Brian said.

"Hey man, do you think I care? I need the strongest cup of Joseph that you got!"

"Do you mean you want a cup of joe?" Brian asked, with saintly patience.

Wallace smacked the counter once more. "I don't have money to pay for it but I'll leave if you give it to me for free."

Brian shook his head. "I told you last time, man. I don't appreciate those threats. If you need a cup of coffee, I'd be more than happy to give it to you on the house."

"Then do it already! La-di-da, la-di-da. Enough singing songs. The only song I want to hear is the sound of pouring coffee. Yum yum I need it now!" Wallace threw his head back and cackled, sending the nervous patrons a couple steps back.

As I watched Wallace wait for his coffee, I felt a warm pang of sympathy in my stomach. Wallace scared me, for sure. And he could be mean. But he was clearly troubled. And few people treated him as kindly as Brian did.

Everyone in the *Brown Cow* breathed a collective sigh of relief upon Wallace's departure. But no one seemed to remember the light-hearted mystery of the sticky notes, until Miss May stepped forward to break the ice. "So do you all want to know who played the practical joke, or not?"

The patrons of the shop turned back to Miss May, with renewed interest on their faces.

Miss May took a step toward the elderly woman who had requested the selfie earlier. "Is that your table by the window? With all the teabags on it?"

The old lady smiled. "Yes. I love tea."

"You've been here quite a while then, haven't you?" Miss May returned the woman's smile.

"You could say that."

"Turn your palms up for me, ma'am?"

The woman complied without remark. Miss May rubbed the tips of the woman's fingers, then my aunt looked up with a grin.

"Just as I thought," Miss May said. "Your fingers are sticky. I felt it when you put your arm around me for our photo earlier. It felt almost like...you'd been handling sticky paper all morning. Would you be willing to open your purse for me, ma'am?"

The elderly woman broke into a broad smile. She opened her purse and inside were hundreds of sticky note pads.

"Show everyone what we're looking at?" Miss May requested. The woman held out her bag and turned in a slow circle for everyone to see. This old lady was the guilty party, and she was proud of it.

The patrons of the *Brown Cow* clapped and laughed, impressed by Miss May's sleuthing.

"Let me guess," Miss May said. "You heard that Chelsea and I come here most weekend mornings. You read it in the Gazette. In one of Liz's articles about us. And you figured you would come by and try to create a mystery for us to solve in real time."

The woman grinned. "That's exactly right, girly. And I saw the sticky note prank online! It just happened to work out perfectly that Brian here is already a fiend for the little yellow squares! How did you know all that?"

"Hunch," Miss May said. "And you've got two issues of the Pine Grove Gazette on your table, both of which are open to articles about Chelsea and me."

More applause rippled through the room.

"Drats," the old woman said. "I did myself in."

"You had help on that front," Miss May said. "Your accomplices? Rita and Willow? They kept shooting looks over to you as I was investigating behind the register."

Rita slapped her knee. "Darn! I gave it away? That's why I can't go to Atlantic City. I've got no poker-face! I say I'm just going to go and watch the Blue Man Group and I end up losing my shirt at the tables. That's it for me! I don't care how blue those guys are. Or how bald! Or how cute!"

"You think the guys in the Blue Man Group are cute?" I asked. "They're all bald and blue."

Rita smirked. "Blue is my favorite color."

I laughed, but my jovial mood faded as I noticed an angry mob marching down Main Street past the shop. I turned to Miss May. "Do you see that?"

Miss May nodded. She ambled toward the main

window, and the other patrons and I crowded behind her. We watched as the angry mob gathered a few storefronts down. They were chanting something but I couldn't make out the words.

Miss May turned to me. "Let's go see what that's all about."

2

BLUEPRINT BLUES

*M*iss May and I hurried toward the angry mob, followed by a few curious patrons from the *Brown Cow*. Including the perp from our recently-solved case, the cute old woman.

As we got closer, I saw that the "mob" was just three or four people, yelling at one man: infamous local real estate developer, Hank Rosenberg.

Hank, early 60's, was tan and bowling-ball-bald. His custom suit strangled his biceps like a python eating a donkey. He grinned as he addressed the crowd.

"You people can moan and groan as much as you want. See the name on that building? Rosenberg. I own it and I can tear it down if I so choose. I'm the golden goose. I lay the golden eggs. All you people, you lay regular eggs. Good for breakfast, maybe. But only worth their weight in eggs."

Arthur, the short and compact owner of the Pine Grove gas station, shoved his way through the crowd like a bull-dozer. "Ingrate! Coward! You need approval to do something like this. It doesn't matter who owns the building."

"And I have approval," Rosenberg said. "From the mayor.

See, me and Linda Delgado? We go way back. Back to the track. Going, going, going gone. End of story."

"Stop talking like that," Arthur said. "Pine Grove is too small for a Massive Mart. You bring something like that here? You'll ruin this town forever."

"Want to know what I think, brother? I think I'm going to need bigger pants after I shove all this new money in my pockets. And I think you're going to thank me for bringing so many jobs to this community."

Teeny pushed her way to the front of the line. "Why are you shoving the money in your pockets? Why don't you get a bank account? You're a crook, that's why!"

"The bank account doesn't matter, Teeny," Arthur said. "What matters is that we already have jobs in this town. We have a florist. And a pizzeria. And a butcher shop. All locally owned. Like they should be. Heck! Right here in this complex we have Big Dan, the best mechanic in all the land. And Master Skinner. His dojo is always packed with karate kids!"

"Get over it, man!" Rosenberg laughed. "You say this town doesn't need a Massive Mart? You say your businesses are successful? Why aren't there more people here to protest? I don't see any 'Master Skinner' here. Do you? And what about this Big Dan clown? He's not here."

"It's Sunday," Arthur said. "Most businesses in Pine Grove are closed Sundays. And that's exactly the kind of small-town atmosphere we're trying to protect."

"That 'small town atmosphere' is the enemy of capital-ism, you fool!" Hank snorted. "My Massive Mart will be open 365 days a year. Including Christmas! Especially Christmas! And it will be the biggest, most beautiful struc-ture this town has ever seen. Imagine it with me... On this very ground will soon be erected the most magnificent shopping mecca in the history of time. Four stories of cinderblock and steel. Three hundred parking spaces illuminated by the brightest lights allowable by law. And inside? A single location where shoppers can procure everything from frozen Tilapia, to tires, to ninety-six rolls of toilet paper in one fell swoop."

"My goodness that is too much TP," the old woman from the *Brown Cow* whispered to me.

"What kind of animal needs ninety-six rolls of toilet paper?" Arthur turned to the rest of the crowd. "If he brings that place here, we're going to lose our local businesses! We're going to lose our homes. And Pine Grove as we know it will be a thing of the past!"

"This conversation is about to be a thing of the past, sir," Rosenberg said. "I'm building the world's biggest swimming pool in New Jersey today. Need to get over there. Tore down an elementary school and a hospital to make space for the pool. It's going to be glorious. Beautiful. The best swimming pool you've ever imagined. You can take a dip there, if you say you're sorry first."

"You can't do this," Teeny said.

Rosenberg shrugged. "This old building comes down in three days. Please direct any further questions you may have to my associate, Sudeer. He's a Pine Grove resident, if you didn't know that already. So at least one person here thinks I'm a genius. Bye now."

Rosenberg climbed into a luxury electric car and hummed away in silence. As soon as he left, every eyeball in the crowd turned to Rosenberg's slight and kindly associate, Sudeer Patel.

Arthur and the others erupted with questions. Sudeer held up his hand to silence the crowd but the protestors only got louder.

The old woman from the *Brown Cow* kept whispering to me as chaos erupted around us. She lamented the state of commercialism in America, the greed of people like Rosenberg, and the wastefulness of paper products. She talked and talked, about how she was so glad she got to visit Pine Grove before the Massive Mart ruined it and how society was spiraling downward. *Or something like that.* OK, I didn't catch a hundred percent of what the old woman said. She talked a lot, and I was distracted by the shouting and contention around me.

After about thirty seconds of utter mayhem in the crowd, Miss May nudged Sudeer aside. She grabbed a nearby milk crate and climbed on top.

"Everybody be quiet!"

Zip. Silence.

"Thank you. Goodness! This is not how we handle our problems in Pine Grove. Arthur. Teeny. You know that. Have we ever done things this way?"

Arthur and Teeny cast their eyes downward.

"I didn't think so," Miss May said. "Now. We're all together on this. So we're going to form a united front. Sudeer, is it true Rosenberg is not going to tear the building down for another three days?"

Sudeer nodded.

"Good. Tomorrow night we've got an open town hall meeting. Just like every Monday night. Let's get organized. Our first step is to convince the mayor that this is a bad idea. If that doesn't work, we're going to keep protesting and we're going to make noise. Liz: do you have contacts in national news?"

Liz, the editor and only reporter of the Pine Grove Gazette, stepped forward. "I went to graduate school with someone who is now the editor of a major national newspaper. He's been following the work I do in the Gazette and he often sends me texts about my great and important work. The man loves a good story. If I give him the scent of this stinky fish? He'll run with it."

"I don't understand what that means," Teeny said. "Can you get national news to pick this up or not?"

"I can and I will." Liz said, standing tall.

"Good." Miss May turned back to the crowd. "Now for the rest of you. Throughout all of this, let's impress ourselves. We must remain civil. And peaceful. And please, can we stop attacking Sudeer?"

"But he's supposed to be one of us," Arthur said. "And he didn't even tell us about this plan. We had to find out about it on Rosenberg's website."

"Sudeer has three little mouths to feed," Miss May said. "No one can fault him for doing his job."

Sudeer sighed. "Actually, baby number four is on the way."

I cringed. *That's a lot of dirty diapers...*

"Hear that?" Miss May said. "This man is about to be a father of four. And he's already exhausted. The dark circles under his eyes have dark circles of their own. Cut him a break."

"Thanks," Sudeer said. "I think."

Miss May patted Sudeer on the back. "Congratulations."

Sudeer mustered a meek smile. It looked like the effort might make him faint.

Miss May turned back to the crowd. "So I'll see all of you at the town hall meeting tomorrow night?"

The members of the no-longer-angry mob nodded.

"Good." Miss May turned to Sudeer. "Tell your boss he better come ready for a fight."

THIRD TURTLE

*M*iss May and I spent much of the rest of the day back at the *Brown Cow*, talking over the plan for the next night's town hall meeting with other members of the community.

The afternoon could have been stressful or disheartening, but it wasn't. Drinking hot cocoa at my favorite coffee shop, surrounded by the impassioned citizens of Pine Grove, I felt happy and at home. Everyone cared so much about preserving the integrity of our town, the scene almost moved me to tears. Of course, I had also recently been moved to tears by a sentimental commercial for liquid cheese, so...grain of salt.

Miss May and I didn't head home for the night until 9 PM. My head hung heavy as she drove up Whitehill Road. But I jolted awake as we pulled up to the farmhouse.

A strange man sat on our front steps, holding something behind his back. I reached out and took Miss May's arm. We had found one-to-three too many dead bodies that year to trust strangers in the dark.

"You know that guy?" I asked.

Miss May shook her head. "Nope."

She trapped the man in the van's headlights and parked the car facing the house. He looked to be in his twenties. Clean-cut. Wearing blue jeans, a denim jacket, and stiff cowboy boots.

"What's he got behind his back?" I asked.

Miss May rolled down the window. "Stay right where you are! Don't move."

The man stood up, keeping one hand behind his back. He had high cheekbones and a bit of reddish-blonde hair poking out from under his hat. And his long, thin frame cast an eerie shadow onto the house behind him.

The man walked toward us.

Miss May honked her horn, long and loud.

The man stopped walking.

She called back out the window. "Put your hands where we can see them."

The man's eyes widened. He shifted slightly but didn't lift his hands. Miss May and I held our collective breath.

"Hands above your head!" Miss May's voice shook.

The man slowly pulled his hand out from behind his back and we saw that he was holding...

...an enormous bouquet of tulips and lilies.

I laughed. "Flowers? What the heck?"

Miss May sighed, relieved. "Come on. Let's go see what he wants."

The man took off his hat and bowed as we approached. "Greetings! I take it from the way you refused to emerge from your vehicle and called out in a threatening tone that my presence gave you a start. Please, allow me to apologize. I'm a gentle creature. Known by many for my warm singing voice and kind demeanor. I mean you no harm. In fact, I'm here to thank you."

The man handed Miss May the flowers, then shook her hand. "My name is Germany Turtle, of the Manhattan Turtles. My parents are the recently deceased Reginald and Linda Turtle, and my uncle is the recently disgraced Dennis Turtle. The two of you, through cunning and genius, apprehended my parents' killer and the dastardly accomplice, and brought them both to justice. I owe you both a deep gratitude. Deeper than the deepest depths of the Mariana Trench. Deeper than the yawning trap of a lion. If you're wondering about that reference, I should explain. I have spent the greater part of the last two years studying lions in Africa. I bonded with them and came to understand myself in ways unimaginable."

"Your parents mentioned that," I said.

Germany Turtle swiveled to me. His hazel eyes crinkled at the corners as he looked at me. Something about the intensity of his gaze sent my stomach into a loop. His voice shifted when he spoke again, like he was meeting his idol. "And you must be the beautiful, inevitable, Chelsea Thomas. I recognize your gorgeousness from the newspaper articles I've read and re-read about you and your aunt. It is from those very same articles that I recognize your pleasing snark, charm, and wit."

I stammered and looked over at Miss May. She grinned. "Chelsea is gorgeous, isn't she?"

Germany remained focused on me. "I'm sorry. I've embarrassed you. For much of my life I worked to get into the habit of dispensing compliments with an easy manner. I forget that sometimes the recipients of my compliments are not ready to accept the genuine praises I want to share. More often than I care to admit, recipients stammer or blush at my remarks. You, Chelsea, are both blushing and stammering now. I take it to mean, therefore, that my compliment struck a chord deep in your heart. But also that you might be uncomfortable."

Miss May laughed. "You're an astute observer of the human condition, Germany."

"Nothing compared to you, Miss May. May I call you that?"

"You can call me anything," Miss May said.

Germany smiled.

"Thank you," I said. "You're very sweet."

"Thank you," said Germany, "for solving the case of the murdered Manhattan Turtles."

In a flourish, Germany reached into a nearby bush and produced an enormous gift basket. A big, cuddly teddy bear sat in the center of the basket, surrounded by several boxes of exquisite chocolates, flowers, and other candies.

He handed me the basket with the deferential bow of the head. "This is for you, Miss Thomas."

I took the basket, and felt my heart thudding a little louder in my chest. *Flattery spiked my pulse, I guess. Yeah, that was it.*

"Wow, Germany," Miss May said. "That gift basket is elaborate, even for someone who did solve the case of your parents' death."

"I must admit, I have fallen head over heels in love with Chelsea, through reading the newspaper articles about her and gazing at the photos of her Venusian form and flowing blond locks. I hope that doesn't make you feel uncomfortable, Chelsea. I am an open person. My parents, as you may have noticed through your dealings with them, had struggles with marital communication. Beyond that, they struggled to connect with other people. Simply put, they despised most people. My act of teenage rebellion was to find good in others. Perhaps that is my natural tendency, and I refused to let Linda and Reginald strangle it from my being. Who can say what prevails in the matter of nature versus nurture? I can tell you, with the lions it is impossible to decipher. No matter. All that is to say, I find that other people are the purest source of joy and beauty in this world and that, of all those billions of sources on the Planet Earth, you are the most pure. For me."

"OK. Wow. That's a lot to take in," I said.

Having spent the better part of the last year orbiting the stoic and hard-to-read — but very attractive — Detective Wayne Hudson, Germany's outpouring of affection was a refreshing, if not bizarre, change of pace. The young Turtle must have read my mind because at that moment, he changed the topic of conversation to Wayne.

"Now, I hope I'm not out of place in declaring my affections. I detected in the newspaper articles that you might be in the beginning stages of a will they/won't they relationship with a large detective. But I did not gather that you are officially entwined, romantically speaking. Therefore, I decided there was no impropriety in my coming here. If I'm incorrect, please inform me. Are you in a relationship with the large detective?"

"She's not," Miss May said.

I shot my aunt a filthy look.

"What?" Miss May said. "You're not."

"We're not official," I conceded. "But you're right. We are in the beginning stages of a relationship."

Germany Turtle nodded and processed the information. After a few seconds, he looked up, eyes as bright as ever. "Well, I just moved into my parents' house in Pine Grove. So I will be here, pursuing you, for the foreseeable future. From what I've heard, the large detective has been out of town for quite a few months."

I shifted uneasily. "He's the star witness in a big trial in New York City."

"I see," Germany nodded. "Not quite the makings of an ideal mate. Being gone for so long."

"If you witness something and have to testify it doesn't make you a bad boyfriend," I said.

"But he's not your boyfriend so it doesn't matter anyway, right?" Germany looked hopeful.

Miss May cracked up laughing. "This kid is sharp!"

"Thank you, Miss May," Germany beamed. "I've received a fine education by all accounts, but according to most tests I am of average intelligence."

Miss May laughed even harder. She clearly loved Germany but that made me hate him, just a little. *Although he did look cute in that cowboy getup.*

"What's with the denim and the boots and stuff?" I asked.

"Yes. I was hoping you wouldn't ask. In what I see now as a misguided attempt to fit in with the suburban culture here in Pine Grove, I donned this denim attire and wore a cowboy hat. Next time you see me, I shall dress in my typical garb. I don't feel comfortable like this, not in my body and not in my mind. More importantly, no one here dresses this way. I was so off-base in my estimation of the vibe in your burg. Did I mention my average intelligence?"

"I don't think it looks that bad," I said.

"So are you interested in me, romantically?" Germany smiled.

I laughed. "I didn't say that."

"Right. Your heart is hovering around the large detective. Well, if he ever makes his way back to town... Tell him he's no longer your only suitor."

I stammered, hunting for the right words with which to

defend Wayne. Miss May, on the other hand, had her words at the ready.

"If she doesn't tell him, I will," Miss May said. "Thanks for the flowers. And the candy."

Once inside the house, in the protected nest of my childhood bedroom, my mind raced with thoughts of Wayne. He had been uncommunicative the past months. But that was because he was a witness on a big case, not by choice. But still...I felt a widening distance between me and Wayne. And Germany's sudden interest made me wish Wayne were more available. As though I had made that wish on a shooting star, my phone pinged with a voicemail. From Wayne.

"Hey Chelsea," the voicemail began. "It's Wayne. Uh. Detective Hudson. I've been busy but I'm thinking about you. It looks like this jury is ready to decide. Should be back in town in a day or two. Call me back?"

I returned Wayne's call. No answer.

Then my eye drifted to Germany's gift basket, waiting under the spotlight of my desk lamp. I grabbed a few chocolates and snuggled under the covers with my worn-down copy of "And Then There Were None," by Agatha Christie.

Even though I knew the ending, the book was riveting. And oh my goodness those were the best chocolates I'd ever had.

In fact, the book and the chocolates had something in common. I ate one chocolate, then another, then another, then a few more.

And then there were none.

4

SMALL TOWN SCORN

I awoke the next morning to the rumbling sounds of a summer storm. Thunder rattled the windows. Rain pattered on the roof like tiny wet feet. Wind chimes sang in chorus on the front porch. I stretched my arms above my head with a small smile.

Ah. What a perfect morning for cinnamon rolls.

When I was little, I had always loved the rain. Every time it drizzled, I would run outside to play. And my mom would lure me back into the house about an hour later with the promise of fresh-baked cinnamon rolls.

I loved watching her pop open those Pillsbury tubes on the counter. I loved the moment the dough burst through the cardboard. And I loved how my mom added extra frosting to the middle roll, just 'cuz I loved that one most.

After my parents died, I had gone to live with Miss May. But she'd continued the cinnamon roll tradition for years, and we always baked a batch from scratch anytime it rained.

On that rainy morning, I snuck down to the kitchen to make the rolls myself. Although Miss May had always been the baker in the family, she had passed many of her skills on to me. And I was excited to surprise her that morning.

To start, I made the basic bread dough that Miss May had perfected over the years. I began with instant yeast so I wouldn't need to pick my nose for hours while allowing the dough to proof. Then I added butter, milk, and eggs. And I made sure I warmed each of the ingredients before adding it to the yeast, an essential step to help the buns rise.

Although Miss May owned a terrific stand mixer, I didn't want to lug it out, so I kneaded the dough by hand. As I massaged the lump of dough, I was careful not to add too much flour and I stopped when the consistency was nice and tacky. It was that tackiness that kept the buns soft when all was said and bun.

Bun pun. Ha. Maybe Germany Turtle was right about my wit.

A few minutes later, I whipped together a quick filling from sugar, cinnamon, and nearly-melted butter. Then I flattened the dough out, spread the filling across the sheet, rolled it up, cut the buns and placed them in the molds to rise.

Next came Miss May's secret ingredient, heavy cream...

Just before I placed the swirled buns in the oven to cook, I warmed a small pitcher of heavy cream and poured it over the dough. The heavy cream would soak into the dough and help the buns rise and stay sticky in the oven.

Miss May and I had tested tons of recipes over the years, and the heavy cream drizzle made our buns taste most similar to the buns you can buy at the mall. The drizzle plumped the buns up and created that rich, creamy fluffiness that was so addictive. And that little extra touch is what sent any normal cinnamon roll over the edge of deliciousness, straight to the cinnamon-flavored moon.

Before long, the smell of cinnamon and dough filled the kitchen and warmed me all the way to my toes. As the rolls baked, I made a quick batch of icing, and brewed a strong pot of coffee. Then the rolls dinged, and Miss May shuffled into the kitchen with a smile.

"Wow. This is a treat."

I smiled. "Rainy day rolls. I wanted to surprise you."

I pulled the cinnamon buns out of the oven and iced them in generous dollops. Miss May leaned over and inhaled the cinnamon scent with a satisfied, "Mmmmmmm."

"They might not be as good as yours," I said. "But they turned out pretty well."

"You shut up," Miss May said. "You know these are better than mine."

A flush of pleasure tingled on my cheeks. "No."

Miss May smacked my arm. "Look at those things! They're straight out of a magazine. An expensive magazine. Like, $7.95 at the checkout!"

I leaned down and inhaled the smell of the cinnamon rolls. Cinnamon, sugar, fresh baked bread... Could anything possibly smell better? "Let's hope they taste as good as they smell."

"I'm sure they do," Miss May said. "So eat plenty, because we've got a long day ahead."

I slid the tray of cinnamon buns onto Miss May's rustic wooden kitchen table and we both sat down to eat.

"What do you mean, we have a long day? Did you get a big order at the bakeshop or something?"

"No big order," Miss May said. "We're hosting an event tonight. I just found out this morning."

I put down my cinnamon roll mid-bite and looked at Miss May. "For real? Does it need custom interior design?

What are we going to do? I should've been working! Not baking stupid cinnamon rolls!"

"Never say that again," Miss May said. "There is nothing more important in life than cinnamon rolls. You hear me? Nothing."

"OK, but really... What are we going to do? And who hosts an event on Monday night? What's going on?"

Miss May pointed out the kitchen window, to the farm. "See all that rain?"

"Yeah. It's a summer storm. My favorite."

Miss May nodded. "Yeah, it's nice and all, but Pine Grove's drainage systems are, how do I put this? Nonfunctional. Town hall got flooded. Lots of places did. So I said we would host the big town meeting in the event barn tonight."

I breathed a sigh of relief. "Oh. OK. So all we need to do is set up the chairs? Maybe a big long table for the town board to sit at?"

"You know me better than that, Chelsea. I want people to feel welcome. I want to make a personal pie for everyone in the audience."

"This is a huge meeting," I said. "There could be a hundred people there."

Miss May smirked. "Like I said. We've got a long day."

By 6 o'clock that night, Miss May and I had baked 100 miniature versions of Miss May's famous "Every Berry Pie." We had also set up folding chairs in the event barn, along with a podium and a folding table for the town board members. I had even managed to string a few market lights from the rafters to give the place a charming glow before the meeting started.

Teeny arrived on the orchard two hours before the meeting began, "to help with the pies." At first, she gossiped with Miss May about Germany Turtle and his "undying love for me." Then she encouraged us to put sprinkles on everything we baked.

But as the meeting drew near, Teeny paced back and forth in the bakeshop like one of Germany Turtle's lions in a cage.

"Teeny. What are you doing? What are you so worked up about?" Miss May asked.

Teeny spun around. "What do you think I'm worked up about, May!? I hate that stupid Massive Mart and it doesn't even exist yet. Who needs 96 rolls of toilet paper? I just don't get it."

"That is a lot of TP," I said.

"It's too many rolls!" Teeny pumped her fist for emphasis. "And I checked out Rosenberg's Massive Mart down-county, by the way. They sell energy bars in packs of four hundred and fifty. What in the world? If I had that much energy, I'd shoot through the roof like a rocket ship!"

"Yeah," I said. "I think you're good on energy."

"What's that supposed to mean?" Teeny asked, her blue eyes bright and suspicious.

Miss May held up her hands to calm things down. "Ladies. Let's stay focused. We're having this meeting to stop Rosenberg. And that's what we're going to do. You don't need to worry about energy bars or toilet paper or rocketships."

"That's what you think," Teeny said. "I haven't told you about the Massive Mart food court yet. They sell French fries and chicken fingers and pizza and pie. All the same stuff I sell. And it's all less than two dollars! And most of it is delicious. I tried it all. It's not fair. How are restaurants like mine supposed to survive? The place sells Christmas trees too, May! And apples. We're all doomed if this place comes to town!"

"Save it for the meeting, Teeny." Miss May squeezed Teeny's shoulder. "You're wasting good stuff here. Great material. The only thing you can do to improve your performance? Muster a few tears. For the newspaper."

Teeny laughed. "I'm more likely to scream than cry. But I'll do what I can."

A few minutes prior to the start of the meeting, the event barn overflowed with angry citizens just like Teeny. Angry, passionate conversation could be heard throughout the room.

Over in the corner, Petunia, the owner of the local flower shop, complained to her friend Ethel. Ethel was hard of hearing, so she kept saying, "Huh!?" But Petunia was so worked up she didn't even notice.

Up at the front of the room, Arthur tried to start various chants, including, "Rosenberg is scum!" And, "Massive Mart is a Massive Fart." For obvious reasons, neither of the chants caught on.

Brian, Rita, and Willow had a hushed conversation along the wall. Rita and Willow wanted Brian to consider moving the coffee shop to another town if Massive Mart opened for business. Brian rejected the idea, citing his love for Pine Grove. Then the girls pointed out that Massive Mart had a coffee shop that sold fifty cent lattes and Brian let out a deep sigh.

Everyone was so unhappy. Even Miss May's individual Every Berry Pies weren't enough to turn the tides of public despair. And to be honest, I was pretty unhappy too. Massive Mart would be way too big for our town.

And if Hank Rosenberg didn't figure that out, I shuddered to think what might happen.

Hell hath no fury like a small town scorned.

5

TOWN GALL

*M*ayor Linda Delgado entered the barn, followed by Hank, Sudeer, and several members of the board.

Petunia heckled as they entered. "Mayor Delgado! Why is Rosenberg with you?"

"No one is with anyone," the mayor said. "Sudeer and Mr. Rosenberg just arrived as we did. That's all."

Petunia and several others booed as Rosenberg took a seat in the front row. The volume of angry conversation rose as members of the crowd joined Petunia as she criticized Rosenberg. But Rosenberg didn't seem to mind the hostility. His condescending smile grew with every remark.

Thirty seconds later, the mayor took her place behind the podium. But the yelling, chanting and booing continued, so the mayor leaned into the microphone and spoke in a commanding voice. "Silence. Now."

From somewhere in the back, Ethel called out, "Say what now?" But other than that, the room fell silent.

"Thank you," Mayor Delgado said. "I understand that we all have a lot we'd like to say. I'd appreciate it if we can remain civil in this process. Many of you are here to discuss the planned Massive Mart at the site of what is now the Rosenberg Building on Main Street. Know that we will get to that, but there are several other issues on the agenda first."

"I know this tactic!" Arthur stood and addressed the crowd. "She wants to drag the meeting out. Make it so we all get tired. She thinks she can bore us so bad we'll leave and give up!"

Petunia stood with a scowl. "I will never give up on this town! Will any of you?"

The members of the audience shouted back a resounding, "No!"

The mayor cleared her throat. "Are you finished, Arthur? Petunia?"

Subtle grumbles of assent flared up from various corners of the room. People tucked into the remnants of the mini pies, trying to calm their nerves with sugar and butter. Not the worst plan.

"OK great," the mayor said. "That was very nice. Now onto our first order of business. Deb Albany has requested the floor."

Deb, a round woman with cat-eye glasses and a thick head of curly hair, got to her feet. She worked as the secretary for the town lawyer, Tom Gigley, but she was famous in town for never shutting up about her vacations and cruises.

That day, however, Deb did not so much as mention her most recent cruise (*we all knew it had been to the Bahamas*). She looked nervous as she took her place behind the podium. And she spoke in a thin, high-pitched voice.

"Hello everyone. I have a personal emergency and I need your help finding my way to a resolution. My kitty cat, Sandra Day O'Connor, is looking for a life partner."

Arthur called out. "For real, Deb? You're making a cat announcement tonight?"

"This is my right, Arthur!" Deb glared, then continued. "Sandra is cute and playful. She has a fluffy, white coat. Deep and soulful hazel eyes. And a long, beautiful tail. She seeks a tomcat serious about joining a committed, monogamous relationship. Sandra would like someone with whom she can share her morning milk. Someone with whom she can watch her favorite cooking and gardening shows. She is open and honest and prefers the same from her mate. Let's get the word out and find a special cat for Sandra Day O'Connor. Thank you and bless you all."

Members of the audience exchanged confused glances as Deb made her way back to her seat.

The mayor had the same confused look on her face as she resumed her place at the podium. "OK. You heard Deb, people. Let's find love for Sandra Day O'Connor, the cat. Moving on. The chief of police has an important message."

I grimaced as I watched Sunshine Flanagan make her way to the podium from the back of the room. Flanagan was Pine Grove's resident hot cop. *Besides Wayne, of course.* She always looked glamorous, like she was the star of her own cop show on TV. Her flowing red hair swoosh-swooshed across her back. Her smile was white and bright. And her giraffe legs carried her across the barn in ten swift strides.

"Good evening, citizens of Pine Grove," Flanagan began.

Petunia stood up. "Hey! Who died and made you the chief?"

Flanagan glared at Petunia so hard I swear I saw one of the fabric lilies on Petunia's shirt wilt. "Chief Daniels retired last month and named me as his replacement. May I continue?"

"Fine. But I'm not sure I like you," Petunia said.

"I can live with that." Flanagan shuffled a few papers around, then looked back up. "OK folks. As some of you may have heard, a burglar broke into a home out near Hastings Pond last night. But I'm here to quash the rumors before they begin. This was not a dangerous break-in. No one was threatened. No one was harmed. And the police are taking care of the matter. So keep living your lives. Keep shopping in our stores and eating in our restaurants. There's nothing to worry about. Thank you."

Liz jumped out of her seat, reporter's notebook in hand. "Flanagan! You can't just walk away from the podium. I've got questions. What did the burglar steal? Whose home was it? Are there any suspects?"

"I'm not at liberty to discuss any further details of the investigation," Flanagan answered.

"Why not?" Liz asked. "You just told us not to worry but you haven't provided any details. Have you asked Chelsea and Miss May for their opinions?"

Flanagan bristled. "The department does not need to consult with amateur sleuths. Not on this matter nor on any other."

"When is Wayne coming back?" Liz asked.

I spoke up without thinking. "Should be in a couple days."

Every eyeball in the room swung to me in unison.

"How do you know?" Liz asked. "Are you and Detective Hudson together now?"

The event barn filled with whispers and giggles. I did not know what to do, so I babbled. *That was my usual move.*

"What? No! That's crazy. Who? Me and Wayne? We're not together. We danced one time. Miss May played a song and we danced to it. It was a slow dance, but I mean, there were still a couple of inches between us. At one point our cheeks grazed. That was nice. Oh man, why am I talking? He's so big and strong. I felt safe in his arms. Can we stop talking about me now?"

All around me, townspeople giggled. So I covered my mouth, closed my eyes, and waited for the moment to end. *Can I be invisible now? Come on, come on, come on...*

The mayor banged a gavel on the podium. "Enough giggling, people! Quiet down. Chelsea's love for Detective Hudson and her weird babbling is not official town business. You can all talk about it after."

Gee thanks, Mayor.

Mayor Delgado cleared her throat. "Now let's talk about the planned Massive Mart at the Rosenberg Building."

Once again, the audience erupted with questions and conversation. But the mayor talked right over the din of conversation and the room quieted down in a matter of seconds.

"I urge each of you to consider the benefits that this kind of store could have within our community," the mayor said. "Every Massive Mart creates hundreds of jobs. Further, Mr. Rosenberg and his associates have agreed to pay significant taxes on this building and business, at a rate far higher than the average Pine Grove business. Also, I have received a guarantee that the Pine Grove Massive Mart will charge less than any other store in the nation for toilet paper."

Arthur stood, red in the face. "What about traffic? What about the impact on other businesses? Also, just for the record, I'm fine with the price on toilet paper now!"

"Me too!" Teeny said. "If you don't like the price, use less toilet paper!"

"And what about Big Dan and Master Skinner?" Arthur asked. "What are they supposed to do?"

Hank Rosenberg laughed and craned his neck to look back at Arthur. "Are we still talking about toilet paper?"

Arthur's eyes bugged out and his cheeks puffed up. He looked like a balloon ready to pop. "No! I'm talking about for life! For their livelihoods!"

Big Dan, owner of *Big Dan's Auto Repair*, stood and raised his hand. "Can I say something?"

A tall man with a goatee and feathery gray hair, Big Dan was well-known as an honest citizen and a great mechanic. So everyone simmered down when he wanted a turn to talk.

"Thanks," he continued. "Yeah. I thought I should say... I'm fine with this."

Mayor Delgado blanched. "You are?"

Big Dan shrugged. "Yeah. Life is about change. I'm bored with being a mechanic. I want to open a donut shop. If that guy Hank tears down my garage? I'll have no choice but to be Big Dan the Donut Man. I don't know how to make donuts. But it can't be harder than building a transmission using spare parts from an old Zamboni."

"Have you discussed this with Master Skinner?" Delgado asked. "Is he also fine with the Massive Mart?"

"I don't talk to that Skinner guy much," Big Dan said. "He's plenty nice. But too intense for me."

"OK," the mayor said. "Thank you for your input, Big Dan. Would anyone else like to speak?"

"How about Rosenberg?" Teeny said. "He's sitting right there, but he hasn't said a word. What's wrong, big fella? Is your suit so tight you're afraid you'll pop a button if you talk?"

Hank Rosenberg stood, still smirking, and took the podium. He leaned in close to the mic so his voice boomed when he spoke. "My associate and I have prepared a statement."

Rosenberg gestured for Sudeer to take the mic.

Sudeer pulled a folded piece of paper out of his pocket and read it aloud. His throat sounded dry and hoarse.

"Rosenberg and Associates is only here as a courtesy. Uh. We... Uh... We are not here to..."

"Louder!" Rosenberg said. "Come on, Sudeer. I don't pay you to dweeb around. Make yourself known!"

Sudeer continued. He did not sound much louder.

"You know what? Forget it. I'll talk." Rosenberg bumped Sudeer out of the way and took the mic. "OK. Hi again, people. Look, I'm only here tonight to engender good will with the people, at the mayor's behest. But we already have her support. And that's all we need. So... I'm going back to my house to eat cheese flavored crackers and scratch myself. Got it? Great. Bye now."

Rosenberg headed toward the exit and the audience erupted in a loud chorus of boos. Rosenberg turned back to the crowd right before he left and took a big, dramatic bow.

And that was the last bow he'd ever take.

6

TAKING THE (BRIEF)CASE

*S*uffice it to say, the people of Pine Grove were not happy with how the town hall meeting went down.

The mayor and Sudeer left right after Rosenberg departed. But the vast majority of those in attendance stayed for over an hour after to discuss possible solutions.

Teeny suggested that we form a human chain and tie ourselves to the Rosenberg Building to prevent the demolition. Arthur suggested we hire our own demolition crew to destroy Rosenberg's house. Big Dan casually surveyed people about their favorite kind of donut, taking careful notes on his phone.

Miss May, meanwhile, tried to keep the whole thing from running off the rails. Miss May was a woman of action. She didn't want to spend any valuable time entertaining the impotent rage of a mob. Unfortunately, that night, not even she had any idea what to do.

When the barn cleared out, I wanted to talk to Miss May. But she looked concerned and distracted. So I cleaned in silence for half an hour as she stacked the chairs, occasionally muttering to herself.

Then, after I couldn't find any other nook or cranny to clean, I crossed to Miss May and asked the Massive Mart-sized question on both of our minds..."Do you think we're going to be able to save the town?"

Miss May let out a deep, long sigh. "I don't know. We only have one business day before those bulldozers arrive. And I'm not sure Rosenberg is a man who can be reasoned with."

"Do you think the Massive Mart will be as bad as everyone thinks?"

"Not necessarily," Miss May said. "Maybe Rosenberg and the mayor are right. Maybe big stores like this are part of progress. The good comes with the bad."

"But a Massive Mart..." I said.

"It's not good," Miss May said. "I know. I'm just trying to see the bright side."

"Other than cheap toilet paper?"

Miss May laughed. "Yes. Other than cheap toilet paper."

I crossed the room to grab a few more folding chairs. And that's when I spotted a briefcase sitting under one of the chairs in the front row.

I grabbed the briefcase and held it up to Miss May. "Someone left this. Any idea who?"

Miss May hung her head and let out a small chuckle. "That's Rosenberg's."

I walked toward her, carrying the case. "It's really heavy. Are you sure it's his?"

Miss May nodded. "I saw him enter with it. We must have had him more flustered than he let on. He hasn't even noticed it's missing yet."

I put the briefcase down on a folding table. Miss May

and I stood over it and neither of us spoke for almost a minute. I wondered if she was thinking what I was thinking.

"He might have sensitive materials in there. Materials that could help us try to get that Massive Mart shut down," I said. "I guess that means we should... return it?"

"What else would we do?" Miss May asked.

I shrugged. "I don't know. Pry it open. Blackmail him? Look for something we can use to stop the demolition?"

Miss May chuckled. "That's crossing a line, Chelsea."

"I know. But so is he."

Miss May picked up the briefcase and handed it to me. "You want to bring it over to him or should I?"

"I'll do it. You go to bed. It's been a long day."

Miss May smiled. "You were up before me, baking cinnamon buns. How about we go together?"

I nodded. "OK. I'll drive."

Five minutes later, Miss May and I were on our way to Hank Rosenberg's house in my sky-blue pickup (which I had purchased from none other than Big Dan).

We called Teeny to see if she wanted to come along for the adventure before we left, but the call went straight to voicemail.

As we drove, it started to rain. Hard. The roads were slippery, not to mention creepy. The air hung heavy with fog and the deluge obscured the road in front of us. Things only got creepier as we neared Rosenberg's mansion.

Rosenberg lived down a long, wooded street in the next town over, and his was the only house on the block. At first the house couldn't be seen through the fog. But as we pulled up the driveway, the home came into view. The place was a two-story, stone castle. Ivy covered the facade and an eerie grey mist circled a turret at the far end.

According to Miss May, this house had been a

monastery in the 19th century and had been abandoned for nearly one hundred years before Rosenberg moved in. Ironic, I thought, that a man so determined to destroy the small-town authenticity of Pine Grove should live in such an ancient home. But I was confident that the irony was lost on Rosenberg. The place was impressive. And that had to be the only reason Rosenberg wanted to live there.

"Does Rosenberg live here alone?" I asked.

Miss May shook her head. "He's married. But I've never met his wife."

As we got closer, I sensed something off with the house. It looked pale and almost like a papier mâché replica. That's when I realized... Rosenberg's castle had been covered in toilet paper. Long sheets of TP were strewn over the trees and across the sloping rooftops. And forty or fifty rolls had been used, if not more.

I parked the car and leaned sideways to get a good look. "Oh my goodness. Do you think someone from town did this?"

Miss May sighed. "I'm sure someone from town did this. Probably an adult. What a disgrace."

"It's kind of funny," I said. "I mean... After all that talk about toilet paper."

"It's not funny. It's juvenile and against the law."

"Hand me the briefcase," I said. "I'll go give it to him."

Miss May shook her head. "No point. Rosenberg's not home. Neither is his wife."

"How do you know?"

"How else could someone have gotten away with all this toilet paper? Besides: no car in the driveway. No lights on in the house."

"OK. So I'll leave it on the front door."

Miss May shook her head. "We can't just leave it there. If

people are willing to TP his house like this? The briefcase won't be safe on the front steps."

"Miss May, come on! It'll be fine! And so what if it gets stolen? We're doing the right thing. We're bringing it here. After that, it's out of our hands."

"But it's in our hands right now. And leaving it unmonitored on an empty stoop is not the right thing."

Miss May glared at me. I hated going out of my way to do a favor for Hank Rosenberg. But I knew she was right. So I clunked the car back into gear and pulled down the driveway.

"Where do we go next?"

Ten minutes later, Miss May and I were parked behind the Rosenberg Building, at the bottom of a hill that Hank planned to turn into a parking lot.

A construction trailer sat at the top of the hill with a light on. But rain poured down, so the path up the hill to the trailer was muddy.

I looked up the hill and cringed. "There's no way my truck's going to make it up that hill," I said. "It's mudslide city. You'd think Rosenberg would put his construction trailer somewhere less precarious. Oh well! Guess we'll just come back tomorrow."

Miss May laughed. "Not so fast. You're wearing your rainboots, right?"

"Yeah. But they're my super cute yellow ones. I don't want to get actual mud and rain on them."

Miss May handed me the briefcase. "Then take ginger steps."

I groaned, took the briefcase, and climbed out of the truck.

Once I got about halfway up the hill to Rosenberg's trailer, the rain slowed. I exhaled in relief, but my respite was short-lived. Seconds after the downpour let up, it returned with doubled intensity. Thunder clapped. Lightning jabbed the horizon in front of me. I liked the rain, yeah. But this was not ordinary rain. And there were no cinnamon buns awaiting me at the top of the hill.

I looked back down at the pickup truck. Miss May was sitting safe and dry inside and every bone in my body screamed at me to turn back, run down the hill and drive away. Except for my sage little pinky toe bone. My pinky toe said, "Keep going, Chelsea! You can do this. Show yourself that you can be brave."

OK, maybe my pinky toe didn't say all that.

The point being, I didn't turn around. I kept trudging up the hill. The next step I took, I slipped and fell onto my elbow in the mud. My elbow shrieked in pain, demanding that I "stop this nonsense right away!" But my pinky toe said, "Nope, you got this! Shut up, elbow." So I got right back up and resumed my trudge.

Boom! Another thunderclap.

I tried not to jump out of my cute yellow rainboots, but it was tough. I could only see a few inches in front of me. And my only reward for making the trek would be the opportunity to face the villainous Hank Rosenberg. Still, the light on in the trailer pulled me forward like, well, a beacon up on a hill.

Boom! Another thunderclap. Another stab of lightning. All I could hear was the sound of my own breath and the persistent, raw melody of the heavy metal blasting from Rosenberg's trailer.

I looked down and stomped my way up the rest of the hill.

Before I knew it, I was face-to-face with the door of the trailer. The heavy metal roared from inside. And it blended with the sound of the thunder to create an unsettling cacophony.

"Hello? Mr. Rosenberg?"

No answer. Just like I expected.

Just like all the other times I had discovered a dead body.

I gulped and shoved that thought away. Rosenberg wasn't dead in the trailer. He had loud music on so he couldn't hear me. It made perfect sense.

Unless he was dead.

"Is anyone in there?"

Metal lyrics. Something about death. Something about revenge. Something about blood spilling on the earth.

My hand reached out and tried the door.

Why did it have to be open?

I opened the door. The music was sounded like a thousand chainsaws singing Christmas carols. And the florescent lighting was so harsh, I had to close my eyes to adjust to the brightness.

After a few seconds, I opened my eyes, stepped inside... and stubbed my toe.

That hurt. But I didn't have time for self-pity. Something was wrong. And I had to find out what.

So I looked up from my throbbing toe and scanned the trailer.

And that's when I saw him.

Hank Rosenberg. Face down in a slice of Miss May's every berry pie.

Not moving. Not breathing.

Not living.

Hank Rosenberg, the most hated man in the history of Pine Grove, was dead.

And he had totally ruined that every berry pie.

7

TRAILER TRAGEDY

I slipped and fell three times running back down the hill toward Miss May. But when I exploded back into the pickup, my aunt was as calm as could be, playing a game on her smart phone.

"Miss May!" I panted, out of breath.

She held up a finger. "One sec. I'm just about to beat this Uzbek woman in Words With Friends."

"Hank." Gasp. "Rosenberg." Gasp. "Rosenberg is-is-is..."

Miss May didn't look up from her phone. "Rosenberg is what?"

I took a few seconds to catch my breath. Miss May looked up at me. We made eye contact. As soon as she saw the look on my face, she knew.

"No!"

I nodded.

Miss May hung her head. "Another dead body? For real!?"

"Everyone. Everyone hated. They hated him." I coughed, still out of breath. Miss May handed me a bottle of water and I took a big swig.

"The toilet paper on the house wasn't enough, I guess." Miss May sighed. "Poor guy."

I hung my head and stared down at my muddy boots. My eyes watered. Miss May put a hand on my shoulder.

"Hey. Hey. It's OK. Look at me. Chelsea. Look at me."

I looked up.

"We'll catch whoever did this. You know that, right? And I already have an idea where we can start."

"You do?" Leave it to Miss May to have a theory before the body was even cold.

"Right after you went in there, someone exited out the back."

My eyes widened. "Wait. What? And you didn't stop them? That person... That's the killer!"

Miss May threw up her hands. "I figured it was a late-night employee or something. And there's no way I could make it up that hill with any kind of speed. Not with my ankles. Knees. Back. Or hips."

"So the killer just..."

Miss May nodded. "They got away."

My face turned white. "They could have gotten me, too. If I had walked into that trailer a minute sooner..."

Miss May grabbed my hand. "Hey. But they didn't get you. Right? You're OK."

I nodded. "I guess so. Yeah."

Miss May shook her head. "I shouldn't have sent you in there alone. You're not my go-for. We're a team."

"It's fine," I said. "You're the brains. I'm the braun." I flexed my bicep. It was a pitiful display but Miss May smiled.

"Did you get a look at the person?" I asked. "Man, woman, young, old? Anything?"

Miss May shook her head. "It could have been Bill

Clinton playing the saxophone for all I know. All I saw was a shadowy figure. That's it."

I pulled out my phone. "Alright. I'll call the cops. Tell them what we—"

Miss May grabbed my arm. "Slow down, Chels. Whoever that was is long gone by now."

"But we can still call the—"

"We will call the cops," Miss May said. "After."

"After what?" I asked.

Miss May took a deep breath. "After I get a look inside that trailer."

Miss May and I climbed back up the hill, one careful step at a time. My body was so pumped full of adrenaline, I navigated the slope with ease.

Miss May, however, struggled. She climbed most of the hill standing sideways with her arm held out in case she fell. After about ten steps she took a break to rub her knees and groan. After ten more steps she took another break, that time to curse her "Irish ankles." But after about fifteen minutes, we made it to the top.

Miss May and I paused when we reached the foot of the trailer. The rain, thunder and lightning had stopped. But the heavy-metal still blasted from inside. And the lyrics were still about death, and vengeance, and blood.

Fun, right?

"I never took Rosenberg for a screeching guitars and pounding drums kind of guy," Miss May said.

"Maybe that's mood music, set by the killer."

Miss May clucked her tongue. "So morbid, Chelsea."

"What? Killers can have panache."

"I guess that's true," Miss May said.

The heavy metal singer belted something about blood coming out of someone's ears.

I swallowed hard. "Can we go inside already? Get this over with?"

Miss May nodded. "I'll go first."

On my initial visit to the trailer my inner sleuth had been overcome by my inner scaredy-cat. So I hadn't taken much time to investigate the crime scene or search for clues.

But when I re-entered the trailer, that time with Miss May, I looked around to take it all in.

The unit was small and rectangular. To the left, a ratty tweed couch, covered in blueprints, hardhats, and tools. To the right, a small folding table. More papers. A plastic cup.

And, oh, that's right. Hank Rosenberg, dead in an Every Berry Pie.

The heavy-metal blared from an old fashioned boombox on the table beside Hank. *Weird, to call a CD player old-fashioned.* But accurate.

Miss May crossed to the boombox and paused the music.

"That's better," she said. "Not that I can't get into a shredding guitar solo, but I don't think that music is appropriate for this moment."

"I don't think it's appropriate for any moment," I said. "But you've always had more adventurous taste than me."

Miss May turned in a slow circle as she surveyed the trailer.

"Pretty empty in here," I said. "Don't you think? Not too many clues. So maybe we can leave?"

"It does seem rather empty," Miss May said. "But this is our one opportunity to check out the scene of the crime before the cops come in and ruin it. We need to be careful. Methodical."

I shivered. "But there's a dead guy right there."

"Which is how I know there are clues in this trailer."

"Like what?" I asked.

"Like there's no back door," Miss May said. "Remember? The person I saw emerged from the back of the trailer. Which means they had to use that window."

Miss May gestured to a window on the far wall. It was small. Maybe two feet high by two feet wide, but no more.

"So our killer is small," I said. "Skinny, probably."

"That means neither of us will be a suspect," Miss May said.

"Hey! I could fit through that window. If I didn't have any arms."

Miss May chuckled. "And that's not the only clue, either. You do the next one."

"I suppose it could be a clue that Rosenberg came here at all. Maybe someone lured him to work after hours. Trapped him here or something."

Miss May shook her head. "Everyone knows that guy was an obsessive workaholic. May he rest in peace. Try again."

I looked around. On second glance, the mess on the couch seemed unnatural. Rumpled papers. Crushed coffee cup. And the couch itself was askew. One end pushed flush against the wall, the other jutting into the room.

"There could've been a struggle. Near the couch."

Miss May nodded. "I agree. But the whole fight didn't happen there."

Miss May crossed back over by the door and squatted to get a look at the wall near the entry. "There's a dent here. About knee-high."

I spotted a similar dent on the opposite wall. "Here's another. And it's fresh. There's plaster on the floor."

"So we're getting a picture of what might've happened here," Miss May said. "Any thoughts on the killer? Gender? Build? Age?"

"We already said they had to be skinny to get out that window."

"Good," Miss May said. "Go on."

"And there was a struggle in the trailer. But there are no signs of forced entry. So whoever left through that window... Rosenberg let them walk in through the front door."

Miss May raised her eyebrows. "Or the person waiting in the trailer when Rosenberg arrived."

"How could they have gotten in?"

"Same way they got out? Maybe that window was open?"

Curious, I walked over to the window. Rainwater had gathered on the floor beneath it.

"That's a good theory," I said. "There's a good amount of water here. Looks like it collected over a few hours, not just the past few minutes."

Miss May smirked. "I know. I saw the water. What else do we know? Or what can we assume?"

"I think the killer was male."

"Why is that?" Miss May asked.

"Simple. They won the fight. And Rosenberg was a big guy. Strong, too."

Miss May crossed to Rosenberg. She squatted down to get a look at his face. Then she circled the body, never taking her eyes off him.

She shook her head. "But Rosenberg didn't die in the fight. There's no blunt force trauma. There's no knife in the back. There are no bullet wounds. I'm not even sure the killer drew blood in that scuffle, and I don't think Rosenberg did either."

"Killer could've cleaned it up."

"True. But look at the couch. The rain. They didn't clean anything else."

"So maybe they argued. Things cooled off. Then... the killer administered poison?"

Miss May shrugged. "Perhaps."

"It's also possible one person made this mess," I said. "I know it looks like a fight... But what if the person who came here upset Rosenberg? Rosenberg punched the wall. He kicked it. He flipped the couch over, then set it right later and tossed all that junk on the cushions."

Miss May smiled. "I think you might be onto something. Are we getting good at this?"

"I think we were already good," I said. "This is just the first time we've gotten such a good look at the scene of the crime."

Miss May nodded. She held the door open for me to leave. "Come on. Let's call the cops."

8

SUN DON'T SHINE

*O*nce Miss May and I made it back down the muddy hill, we called the police.

Hercules, a young officer I had gotten to know on our previous case, answered. He said Chief Flanagan would be up in a few moments.

Hercules also asked if we knew any eligible bachelor-cats for Sandra Day O'Connor, but we did not. Apparently Sandra-the-cat's love life was official police business in Pine Grove. And that did not surprise me.

Miss May and I retreated into the warmth of my pickup truck to wait for Flanagan to arrive. Though we were both distracted — for obvious reasons — we tried to make conversation.

Miss May and I talked about the history of Pine Grove. We complained about the rain, which Miss May described as "angel urine." And we lamented that Rosenberg had face-planted to his death in one of Miss May's hand-crafted pies. Callous, but true.

Then the conversation turned back to our budding investigation.

"You know what I was just thinking?" Miss May said. "We have one more big clue we have not yet investigated."

I looked over at her. "What's that?"

Miss May smirked. "Rosenberg's briefcase. No one knows he left it at the orchard. Once we get home, we can crack it open and see what we can learn."

My eyes widened. "Oh. Shoot."

"What?"

"I left the briefcase up in the trailer."

Miss May grabbed her head. "Chelsea! You did? Why?"

Sirens sounded in the distance. Doubtless, Flanagan on her way to the trailer.

"You have to go get it!" Miss May said.

"But Flanagan is on her way! Plus, I'm not sure that's right. Isn't it kind of stealing?"

"We're not stealing it, we're borrowing it. In the name of justice," Miss May said. "Think about it. Who do you suppose will use the contents of the briefcase more wisely? Us or the police? Who has a better chance of using that briefcase to bring closure and dignity to Rosenberg's death? Who has a better shot at finding the killer?"

I bit my lower lip. "I mean, I feel like I should say the police but you want me to say us."

"It's obviously us," Miss May said. "We've already solved..." She counted on her hands, then gave up. "We've already solved a bunch of murders! The police haven't solved any!"

"But what if—"

"If it's personal stuff that doesn't relate to the murder we'll drop it off with Rosenberg's wife. We'll tell her we found the briefcase under a chair when we were cleaning up after the meeting. Which is true!"

The sound of Flanagan's approaching sirens grew louder, and I knew I had to move.

"OK," I said. "I'll go get the briefcase. But if I get caught—"

"You won't. Go!"

I darted up the hill for the third time that night as the wail of Flanagan's cop car drew nearer and nearer.

Once I reached the peak, I could see out over all of Pine Grove. The twinkling lights below seemed almost like a mirror image of the stars above. Pine Grove could be transcendent after a big summer rain. I would have loved to take a deep breath and soak up the beauty. But I could see the red and blue bulbs of Flanagan's squad car from my perch. And she was coming at me. Fast. So I glanced around to make sure the coast was clear, then slipped into the trailer.

I muttered as I scanned the room, hunting for the briefcase. "Come on. Where are you? Little brat. Bratty briefcase." I spotted it over on the couch. "There. Got ya!"

Three quick steps and I had the goods in my grasp. A few more steps and I was back outside.

I shot a quick glance back toward the flashing red and blue lights. From the looks of it, Flanagan's cop car was less than a block away. Then I looked at the pickup truck, all the way at the bottom of the hill. There was no way I could walk down that muddy hill and hide the briefcase before Flanagan arrived. So I did the next best thing...

I found the slipperiest section of the hill, got a running start, and slid down on my backside, holding the briefcase above my head like it was a newborn child.

For the first second, it was a fun ride. Then I felt the gravel scraping against my rear, and it got less fun. But the mudslide did the trick.

I stashed the briefcase under some farm equipment in

the bed of the pickup, bid a silent adieu to the seat of my
ruined pants, and turned around just as Flanagan squealed
to a stop beside my truck.

Flanagan climbed out of her police car one long leg at a
time, like she was the star of a sexy 80's music video. Her red
hair swish-swished across her back as she looked from side
to side, surveying the landscape with a swift, brutal gaze.

I tried to wipe the mud from my pants, but I just
smudged it around even more. I took a deep breath. I probably looked like I was wearing a dirty diaper, but that was
just going to have to be OK. I mustered my best nonchalant
smile and waved to Flanagan. "Sunshine! You made it! We
could have used a little more of you on days like today."

"It's Chief Flanagan. Thank you very much. And what
you mean 'days like today'? Rainy days? Or days on which
you find a dead body? They seem to happen with almost
equal frequency."

My smile faltered. "Both, I guess."

"Well now it's night. Everyone knows the sun doesn't
shine at night except during the summer in Alaska,"
Flanagan said with absurd seriousness. "Do you want to tell
me what happened here?"

Miss May stepped out of the pickup truck. "Hi there,
Sunshine!"

"It's Chief Flanagan. Thank you very much."

Miss May nodded. "Chief. Right. Almost forgot. Congratulations."

Flanagan glared. "Uh-huh."

Miss May kept right on smiling. "Hey, why don't you
jump in the pickup? We can talk out of the rain."

"Or the two of you could climb in the back of the squad
car. I could take you down to the station. Toss you in the
interrogation room. We could talk there."

"The rain has lightened up," Miss May said. "Outdoors is fine."

Flanagan nodded up at the trailer. "So Rosenberg is up there? Dead?"

Miss May and I nodded.

"And what were you two doing here so late at night?"

Returning his briefcase.

Shoot. Can't say that.

I turned to Miss May, expecting her to have an answer. She was usually quick on her feet, despite her bad hips, knees, ankles and back. But that night she had nothing but a stammer and gulp.

So I came up with an excuse of my own. "We came to apologize to Mr. Rosenberg. For how the meeting went."

Flanagan's nostrils flared. "Why? It wasn't your fault."

"Still. We were the hosts of the evening, and our other guests treated Mr. Rosenberg unfairly. That's bad hospitality. Worse yet, bad business. So we came by to set things right."

"And when you got here Rosenberg was dead?" Flanagan looked from me to Miss May. "Is that true?"

Miss May recovered her voice and straightened her shoulders. "Every word."

Flanagan directed us to wait outside as she inspected the trailer. Five minutes later, she emerged, tucking her notebook into her back pocket.

"Good news, ladies."

Miss May looked over at me, then back to Flanagan. "Good news... how?"

Flanagan stood tall. "That man died of natural causes."

"Are you certain?" Miss May asked. "That place was a mess."

"Didn't seem so bad to me. Standard construction trailer.

Bound to end up with some dents and dings. Part of the territory."

"But Rosenberg was an impeccable man," Miss May countered. "Just look at the suits he wore."

"These contractor guys have their public persona and then they have their work persona. They're all gruff. They're all sloppy. No exceptions. That trailer looks just like every construction trailer I've ever seen."

"Every construction trailer you've ever seen has dents in the wall?"

Flanagan nodded. "Yup. My father worked construction his entire life. Have you been in many of these trailers? Didn't notice one on your quaint little apple orchard."

"Well…"

"And weren't you a lawyer before you took over the orchard? Not a lot of construction trailers in that line of work, either."

Miss May's career as a former prosecutor in New York was a frequent topic of conversation, in that Miss May liked to preface sentences with, "When I was a prosecutor in New York City…" On our last case, Wayne had thrown some shade on Miss May's current standing with the NY bar. When I'd tried to dig deeper on whether or not Miss May still had a license to practice law, she'd shut me down.

Another mystery that would have to wait for another day.

"I know what the inside of a construction trailer looks like," Miss May said. "More importantly, I know how to recognize the signs of the struggle. I know how to recognize when someone has been murdered. Or have you forgotten? Chelsea and I solved the last several murders in this town. No thanks to you or your squad."

"That's not how Detective Hudson tells it. The way he

tells it, he ran point on those cases. The two of you got in his way. Jeopardized several dangerous operations."

"Wayne has to say that stuff when he's on the record," I said. "He knows how much we've helped. And he appreciates it."

Flanagan laughed. "Maybe he appreciates the slow dance, Chelsea. But trust me. He does not appreciate you or your meddlesome aunt."

"You think he appreciates you?" I snapped. "You were an OK detective. But now that you're chief? This whole town is in danger." My nostrils flared. I was mouthing off to the police chief, which was stupid. But she was declaring this a natural death, which was even stupider.

"Are you finished?" Flanagan's tone was cooler than soft-serve straight out of the machine.

"No," I said. "I won't be finished until whoever did this to Rosenberg is behind bars."

Flanagan got in my face. "This was not a murder. Do you hear me? You stay out of it."

"How can you say this was not a murder?" Miss May asked. "There were signs of a struggle. Rosenberg was the most hated man in town. The back window was open. Heavy metal was blasting on the stereo."

Flanagan turned on Miss May. "I didn't hear heavy metal."

Miss May didn't miss a beat. "We turned it off when we arrived. So we could hear if Rosenberg was breathing."

"So you tampered with evidence at the scene of a crime," Flanagan said. "I should take you in for that."

Miss May crossed her arms. "You said there was no crime."

"Exactly," Flanagan said. "The last thing this town needs is another murder. Our businesses are suffering."

"My orchard is doing just fine. Even better since the murders, actually." Miss May shrugged. "Tourists with a morbid curiosity, I guess."

"Forget the tourists," Flanagan said. "I'm talking about locals. The mayor's all over me about it. Residents don't feel safe. They don't want to walk the streets. Apparently it's my job to force the people of Pine Grove to shop in our stores and not on the Internet."

"So that's why you're declaring this an accident," Miss May said. "And that's what you were going on about at the meeting. Acting like a home-invasion is no big deal. The mayor is pressuring you to keep up an illusion of safety in Pine Grove. For economic reasons."

"I'm declaring Rosenberg's death an accident because it was an accident," Flanagan said. "End of story."

"You are ridiculous!" Miss May laughed. "You know what's worse for business than a murder? A police force that lets murderers roam the streets."

Flanagan took a step toward Miss May and stared down my aunt with an imposing glare. "My department values nothing more than the safety of the good people of Pine Grove. Hank Rosenberg was not murdered. There will be no investigation. Not by me. Certainly not by you and your little niece. So stay out of my way."

Flanagan swung her gaze to me. "I'm warning you too, Chelsea. I'm not Detective Hudson. I don't take kindly to interruptions. And I'm not nearly as good of a dancer."

Flanagan stormed down the hill without slipping or sliding even a little on the muddy earth.

Half an hour later, a coroner took Rosenberg's body away. And all that remained was the mystery of who killed him.

And why.

9

LAND AND PLEAS

*K*P opened the door to his cabin and rubbed sleep out of his eyes. He wore flannel pajamas. And the toes of his slippers had googly eyes and a little frock of hair. He groaned when he saw us. "What the heck are you two girls doing here at this abominable hour?"

"Can you keep a secret?" Miss May asked.

"You know I can keep secrets, May. You want me to list all the secrets I've kept for you over the years? Or do you want to tell me why you're here so I can get back to my beauty rest."

Miss May leaned forward. "Can we come in?"

KP eyed Rosenberg's briefcase. "It depends. That thing filled with money?"

"We have no idea," I said. "That's what we need to talk to you about."

"I don't know what's in there!" KP grumbled.

"No one does," I said. "That's the issue."

KP looked from me. To Miss May. To the briefcase. Back to me. Then he stepped aside, and we entered his cabin.

Like the cabins we rented to guests, KP's was small and

homey. All dark wood and big windows, with a functioning fireplace along the far wall. But KP had decorated his place differently than I had decorated the guest cabins.

KP's cabin, for instance, featured quite a few mementos from his time in the navy. My favorite piece was an old, iron anchor propped up on the mantle. His cabin also featured a 65-inch TV, a big Casablanca poster and a signed basketball from the 1998 Kentucky Wildcats.

KP took a seat on his tattered couch and Miss May and I plopped down on either side of him.

He patted the coffee table. "OK," he grunted. "Let's see what you got."

"That's the problem." Miss May thunked the briefcase on the table. "We don't know what we've got. Because we can't get this thing open."

KP chuckled. "Now hold on one pretty little second. Why would the two of you be in the possession of a locked briefcase, but not have the key?"

"And you've discovered the secret we need you to keep." Miss May looked sheepish.

KP perked up, excited. "I'll be! Don't tell me you and little missy over here stole this thing?"

"We didn't steal it," I said. "We just failed to return it to its owner. And now we need you to open it."

"Whoa Nelly. Yes, I may have a troubled history with the local library's outrageous overdue fees. But I'm no common criminal. I'm not a jewel thief!"

"I'm not saying you're a jewel thief," Miss May said. "I doubt there are jewels in the briefcase. But I've seen you jimmy the lock on the farmhouse. Remember? That time I got locked out. And that other time. And that other time."

KP turned to me with a smile. "You know, for a top

sleuth, your aunt can't seem to figure out where she puts her own keys most days."

"I know," I said. "I've suggested gluing them to her hand."

KP guffawed and slapped his knee.

"Enough already," Miss May said. "This isn't bully Miss May Day, KP. Will you help us or not?"

"Those locks on the farmhouse are easy. A blind monk could pick 'em with his pinky finger. This here... This is a whole different story. I'm going to need more information before I agree to a project like this."

Miss May sighed. "What do you need to know?"

Thus began the onslaught of questions.

KP wanted to know everything about the briefcase, so we told him. Then he wanted to know about the trailer. And the dead body. And Flanagan. So we relived the whole stressful, muddy evening in great detail.

Then he wanted to know what brand toilet paper had been used to vandalize Rosenberg's house. And that's where Miss May drew the line.

"I can't tell toilet paper brands just by looking at the squares," Miss May said. "Now will you help us or not?"

KP laughed. "I was wondering when you were gonna put your foot down! You let me get in a lot of questions."

Miss May glared. KP threw up his hands in surrender. "OK, OK, yes. I can help you open the briefcase. But not tonight."

Miss May stood in a huff. "What do you mean, not tonight?"

"It's late," KP said. "Or early, depending on how you look at it."

"Yeah and it got even later since we spent the last hour answering your questions!" Miss May crossed her arms.

KP shrugged. "Don't get your Dockers in a ditch, lady. I couldn't crack this case tonight if my life depended on it. I need special tools. I'll pick them up in the morning."

Miss May sighed. "You can get it open tonight, KP. I know you can."

"I cannot, May. Not unless you want me to strap fireworks to the thing and send it to the moon. But that'd bring that new police chief over here faster than you can say 'you need a permit for those fireworks in this county, sir.'"

"OK," Miss May said. "First thing in the morning. Promise?"

KP smirked. "Cross my heart and hope to die."

The next morning, KP got to work on opening the briefcase. Miss May and I hovered over him as he worked, but KP didn't seem to find our presence all that useful. In fact, he threatened to quit and flee to Turkmenistan if we didn't leave him alone. So we went to *Grandma's* for some breakfast.

Granny was nose-deep in her newspaper when we arrived. But the door chimed as we entered the restaurant, and she looked up.

"Table for two?"

I stammered. That was one of the first and only times I'd ever heard the matriarch speak and her smooth, commanding voice surprised me.

"Table for two would be great," Miss May said. "Thanks."

Granny nodded and swung her legs off her stool. But before Granny's ancient feet reached the ground, Teeny hurried out of the kitchen and bustled toward us. "What are you two doing here?"

"What do you mean?" Miss May asked. "We're doing

what we always do. We're coming for breakfast. Oh, and we wanted to fill you in on a new case." Miss May smirked. Teeny loved being involved in investigations, so it was always fun to share the scoop with her.

"New investigation. Yippee! Wait. Aw. Who died?" Teeny took a step closer to Miss May. "I hope it was that rude old woman who works at *Ewing's Eats*. She refused to give me my extra sprinkles the other day. Tried to charge me sixty more cents!"

"So you wish death upon her?!" I exclaimed. "That seems harsh."

"Trust me, you didn't hear her tone," Teeny said.

"It wasn't the *Ewing's* lady," Miss May said. "And you should really cut back on the sprinkles. And try to be less vengeful."

"Don't tick me off and you'll be fine," Teeny said. "Anyway, who croaked? Is it a scandal? Is there intrigue? Do you need my expert insight and investigative prowess?"

"We might need you, yeah." Miss May eyed Teeny's jacket and purse. "But are you headed out? We wanted to talk now."

"I'm just going over to have breakfast at Petey's new restaurant. I promised him I'd go but I've been too busy. Come with me!"

"I can't believe Petey opened his own restaurant," I said. "It seems like just yesterday he was that high school dropout you were nagging to get his degree."

"That did happen yesterday," Teeny said. "And I was right. From what I've heard Petey's new place isn't attracting many customers."

"It's too expensive," I said. "People in Pine Grove don't want to break the federal bank for a night out, unless they're going into the city for a special occasion."

"I think our town is more than ready for a fancy restaurant," Miss May said. "I'd love to join you for breakfast. Chelsea? What do you think? Can we get Teeny up to speed over at Petey's place?"

I wrinkled my nose. "Do you think he has at least one variety of fried potato?"

"If he doesn't I'll jump back in the kitchen and make some," Teeny said.

I laughed. "I'm sure he'll appreciate that."

Just like that, off we went to Petey's new restaurant.

Peter's Land and Sea was all the way up a hill outside of town, nestled onto the first floor of a large Revolutionary War era home. The building was beautiful. Two stories. White with charcoal gray shutters. And it had a sprawling backyard with a gazebo that would be perfect for weddings and other occasions.

Miss May, Teeny, and I walked the mile or two up to the restaurant. For the first ten minutes, Miss May and I filled Teeny in on the details of Rosenberg's death. Then we started our way up the hill to the restaurant, and the conversation halted so we could huff and puff to the top.

When we made it to the peak of the hill, we were sweaty, out of breath, and hungry.

As we entered, I stopped to look at the restaurant's signage. "*Peter's Land and Sea*. That's an interesting name."

Miss May shrugged. "Seems a bit basic for such a fancy place."

"What do you suppose it means?" Teeny asked.

"I think it means what it says," Miss May said. "They serve land food and seafood."

"Land food?" Teeny said. "That's everything other than fish."

"Basic," Miss May replied. "Like I said."

"So is my restaurant technically a land food restaurant?" Teeny asked.

"Nope," Miss May said. "You serve shrimp poppers on your appetizer menu. So that's land and sea. Just like this place."

Teeny beamed. "I knew it. I taught this kid everything he knows."

The second we entered the vestibule, Petey rushed toward us with his arms spread. As he got closer I noticed a tiny mustache on his upper lip. I almost laughed out loud but disguised it with a cough at the last second. A gleeful, amused cough. Which probably fooled no one.

"Teeny! Miss May. Chelsea. Welcome to *Peter's Land and Sea*. It is my privilege to have you."

"It's a privilege to be here, Petey," Miss May said.

He leaned in. "What do you think of my mustache? Too much?"

"Just enough," I said. "Very European."

"OK, good," Petey said. "I'm going for that 'French Mime who discovered a love for cooking and opened a hit restaurant' look."

"Nailed it," I said.

Petey turned to Miss May and Teeny. "What do you two think? French mime who can cook? Or teenage loser with a bad mustache?"

"The first one," Teeny said. "Très cool."

"Agreed," Miss May said. "Too cool to be a mime. Just cool enough to be a five-star chef."

Petey breathed a sigh of relief. "OK cool. 'Cuz I think the dishwashers are calling the 'stache ugly in Spanish."

"I'm sure that's not true," I said. "Why do you think that?"

"Whenever I enter the kitchen they laugh and use their fingers to make little mustaches on their lips."

"Yup. They're making fun of you," Miss May said. "But who cares! Look at this place. You have your own restaurant. That's amazing!"

Petey looked over at Teeny. "Do you think it's amazing too?"

"That depends," Teeny said. "Do you serve French fries?"

Petey laughed. Teeny looked at him over her sunglasses. "I'm not joking, kid."

"Oh," he said. "Right. Uh. We offer steak-frites with several dinner options."

"Steak-frites. That's French for fried potatoes, right?" Teeny asked.

Petey nodded.

"Then whip us up a batch! This is my new favorite restaurant!"

As soon as Petey led us to a table and walked away, Teeny leaned in and whispered. "I didn't see a mustache. Did you?"

I laughed. "It's there. If you really look."

"Do you have to make your eyes blurry?" Teeny asked. "Like one of those books of magical illusions?"

I shook my head. "Next time stand real close. You'll see it."

Teeny sighed. "I hope this place survives. Petey is such a hard worker. Remember when I used to make him scrape the gum off every table in the restaurant? He never complained once."

Miss May looked around. "Kind of empty in here though."

Teeny shrugged. "People lined up around the block to

eat his food when I let him take over the kitchen at *Grandma's*."

"I remember," I said. "And that food was good. Especially the fries."

"I can't wait for those fries." Teeny rubbed her hands together. "I can't wait to learn more about this mystery, either."

"We told you pretty much everything on the walk," I said. "Oh! Except for the briefcase."

Teeny gasped and covered her mouth. "There's a briefcase? What's in it? Secret files? Photos of Russian spies? Cash money millions? All hundos? Unmarked? Now we're talking!"

I laughed. Then, over the next few minutes, we answered all of Teeny's questions. We also ate a giant mountain of delicious fries, then ordered another. And by the time we finished with our second helping, Teeny was all caught up.

"Wow," she said. "Dead developer. Aloof chief of police. Signs of a struggle. A shadowy figure who disappeared into the night... This is the best case yet. A classic whodunit."

"Try not to be so gleeful," Miss May said. "Someone died."

"You think I'm going to cry the Hudson over Hank Rosenberg?" Teeny said. "I hated that guy. Everyone knows I hated that guy. Ah! Am I a suspect?"

"Considering that no one is investigating except for us, I think you're safe," Miss May said. "Although I should ask... Did you kill Rosenberg?"

"How dare you, May," Teeny said, aghast.

"I mean, you did want the waitress from *Ewing's* to die a horrible death because she deprived you of sprinkles," I said.

"I did not kill Hank!" Teeny said. "Although I am small enough to have gotten out that window. But do I know enough about poison to kill the guy without using a weapon? I do have access to lethal kitchen chemicals. Oh no! Now I'm questioning myself."

"Yeah," Miss May said. "Save those questions for our actual suspects. And try to keep it down. Petey is coming over."

We all turned in unison as Petey approached, carrying three dishes capped with silver covers.

"Ladies. Your breakfast is served."

"Oh," I said. "I think this might be the wrong table. We only ordered the fries. Twice."

"Don't be silly," Petey said. "I want to serve you the full breakfast."

"Still," I said. "We haven't ordered."

"The customers at my restaurant don't order for themselves. I make one dish every day and serve that to everyone. That's how they eat in Japan."

Teeny, Miss May, and I exchanged glances. Then, Petey served each of us with a flourish. When he uncapped my dish, it surprised me to see what appeared to be a luxurious egg and cheese sandwich on a plain bagel.

"This looks delicious," I said. "Did you say this food is Japanese?"

Petey hung his head. He rubbed his temples. "OK. Fine. Fine! I'm a fraud. You caught me!"

Petey sat down at our table and buried his head in his hands. His voice wavered as he spoke. "I'm working hard at this place. I am. But this business is impossible. Customers are so rude. Not you guys. Other people. And cooking every day is hard! Plus, my place got broken into last night. Someone stole all my farm-to-table produce. Two boxes of tomatoes. A hundred dollars' worth of bok choy. They even took my sweet potatoes! And those farm to table vegetables are so expensive. I don't get it. It's just from a farm! Isn't all food technically from a farm? When did farms get so fancy?"

Miss May looked at me and Teeny, then back to Petey. "It's OK, Petey," Miss May said. "You're going to be fine."

"And I really love your mustache!" Teeny added.

"I am not going to be fine," Petey said. "I'm a failure. And my mustache is ridiculous! I just shaved it in the bathroom!"

Teeny placed a comforting hand on Petey's back and sneakily squinted at his upper lip. She looked at me and mouthed, "I can't tell the difference!" Then she turned back to Petey. "Hey. It's OK. This place will be a huge success. I know it. It just takes time."

Petey looked up. "You think?"

Teeny nodded. "Of course! You just caught some bad luck. Did you call the police about your stolen ingredients?"

Petey jutted his lower lip out. "Chief Flanagan said they don't have time to investigate stolen lettuce."

"Doesn't sound like they investigate anything," I said.

"What does that mean?" Petey asked.

"Um. Well..." *Shoot. Why did I so often talk when I had nothing to say?*

Thankfully, the restaurant phone rang and bailed my loose lips out of a tight bind.

Petey stood up. "I should get that. I hope it's a giant order. But it's probably just one of my friends. They prank call me every hour on the hour. It's a lot of fun. For them."

Petey trudged away and Miss May, Teeny, and I exchanged glances.

Petey's distress worried me. And I was even more

worried about Pine Grove. Murders? Break-ins? Whatever happened to peaceful small-town living?

I was on the verge of a panic attack. But then I took a bite of Petey's egg and cheese bagel and it transported me to a beautiful, serene place.

It was the best sandwich I had ever tasted. The cheese was melty, the eggs were rich and fluffy. And the bagel, in true New York style, was chewy yet soft. I let out a loud, involuntary moan and took another bite.

If only we can catch Rosenberg's killer, I thought, *this egg sandwich would make me the happiest woman in the history of human kind.*

But that was a big if. And it scared me.

So I took another bite.

10

WATER FOUNTAIN CHATTER

*M*iss May swallowed her last bite of sandwich, then let out a deep sigh of satisfaction. "OK. Now that those sandwiches are out of the way and safely in my stomach, we can discuss Rosenberg's death."

Teeny perked up. "Wait! I have a question."

Miss May glared.

"It's important!" Teeny said.

"OK, T. What's up?" Miss May asked.

"You two are definitely taking the case, right?"

Miss May nodded. "At this point, we're sleuths. It's in our bones."

"OK. Because I can talk you into it, if you need me to."

Miss May shrugged. "You don't have to talk us into it."

"Are you sure? Because I will, if you need that," Teeny's eyes lit up. "I can be motivational. Remember last time?"

"Last time KP was in jail. That's why we got involved," Miss May said.

"Not true," Teeny said. "You weren't going to take the case. But I convinced you. I motivated you with my personal brand of fiery enthusiasm. I instilled in you the confidence that you carry with you to this day."

Miss May shrugged. "If you say so."

Teeny jutted her lower lip out. "Why can't you just say I'm an integral part of the team?"

I laughed. "Miss May's messing with you, Teeny. I don't know what we would do without your personal brand of fiery enthusiasm."

"Really?" Teeny asked.

I nodded.

Teeny smiled. "In that case, let's talk suspects. I'm thinking it was that crazy guy, Wallace the Traveler. He scares the deer corn out of me. And I've heard him threaten to kill several people."

· · ·

"Yeah, I heard him threaten a puppy once," I said. "Apparently it looked at him 'all cute-like' and Wallace didn't appreciate that. But I don't know if we can suspect a guy just because he's got a few screws jumbled up in his head. I mean... Did you ever hear Wallace say anything bad about Rosenberg? Did he and Rosenberg argue in public? Anything like that?"

"No," Teeny said. "But it's kind of a big coincidence. This Wallace guy shows up in town. A few weeks later, Rosenberg is dead."

Miss May sipped her water. "That's a good point. But why would Wallace have waited a few weeks before killing Rosenberg?"

"The creep-o Wallace probably needed time to hatch a plan," Teeny said. "Seems to me, he studied Rosenberg's habits. Knew when Rosenberg would be alone in the trailer. Waited for the right moment. And pounced!"

"Not a bad theory," Miss May said. "And I like that you didn't steal it from an episode of *North Port Diaries*."

"Oh no, that theory is straight from *NPD*," Teeny said. "Season nine, episode eleven. Number thirty-five of my top fifty episodes of all-time."

"Aren't there only fifty episodes total?" I asked.

. . .

"There are forty-four but I count a few of them twice because they're so good," Teeny said.

"I think that's the number of suspects we have on this case," I said. "Everyone in town hated Rosenberg. And they hated that Massive Mart even more."

Miss May nodded. "But who had the most to lose if the store opened?"

"We all did," Teeny said. "Massive Mart would have put every small business owner in Pine Grove into the poor house."

"That might be a slight exaggeration," I said. "But you're right. And it would have been even worse for Big Dan and Master Skinner. Both their businesses are in the Rosenberg Building!"

"Big Dan couldn't care less," Teeny said. "He's already got one foot in the donut shop. Plus, he's got a great beard."

Miss May shook her head. "Have you been checking out Big Dan's beard?"

Teeny shrugged. "The man has a well-groomed face."

I smirked. "Sounds like someone might have a crush."

"Oh hush up," Teeny said. "I thought this was a murder investigation, not a water fountain."

I cocked my head. "Water fountain? What do you mean?"

"Water fountain," Teeny said. "That's where people gossip. Everybody is always talking up a storm at the water fountain."

Miss May and I exchanged a confused look.

"I think you mean a water cooler," Miss May said.

Teeny waved her off. "Oh you get what I mean. People drink water and talk trash. Now can we get back to the murder theories?"

"Sure," Miss May said. "I think you made a good point about Big Dan."

"You also love his beard?" I asked.

"No, Chels, I'm talking about his motive," Miss May said. "Big Dan didn't care about the Rosenberg building. So he didn't have much reason to kill Rosenberg."

"Master Skinner is no killer, either," I said. "That was a fundamental tenet of his teachings. Martial arts are not for violence."

Teeny gnawed on a fingernail. "That sounds like a nice philosophy. But Master Skinner has an inner darkness, if you ask me. And he was missing last night. How did you say Rosenberg died? Is it possible he had been karate chopped to death?"

"It was hard to tell," Miss May said. "Didn't seem to be any signs of blunt force trauma but I guess an expert karate chop could have gone under my radar."

"That's ridiculous!" I said. "I'm telling you, Master Skinner has achieved inner peace through years of karate and meditation. He is one with the universe."

"There was evidence of a struggle in that trailer,

Chelsea," Miss May said. "Master Skinner is one of the only people I know who would be strong enough to dent that wall. And he could also fit through the window. He's a lithe and compact man."

"But you said it seemed like Rosenberg made that mess by himself!"

"And I still think that's possible. But the facts—"

I slammed my hand on the table. "Skinner didn't do it! Trust me."

Miss May and Teeny looked at me like I was being obstinate.

"Look," I said. "I just... I looked up to Master Skinner a lot when I was a kid. And my instincts tell me he couldn't have done this. If any real evidence points to him? Fine. We can go question him. But isn't there anyone else we can talk to first?"

"I think he's guilty," Teeny said. "But whatever. Who else is on the list?"

"What about Flanagan?" I asked. "It's odd she's choosing not to investigate. There's so much reason to suspect foul play."

"That's a good point," Miss May said. "Chief Flanagan may have had a hand in this."

"But do you think she could have sneaked out that window and gotten back to her cop car in time to drive away, get our call, and return to the scene of the crime in a few minutes?" I asked.

Miss May shrugged. "It's not likely. But it's possible. And you're right... It is odd that she's chosen not to investigate this as a murder."

"Maybe Flanagan is working on the mayor's orders," I said. "Sounds like Delgado wants Flanagan to keep the murder numbers down."

"That would make sense," Miss May said. "At the rate we're going, Pine Grove will have more murders per capita than the south side of Chicago."

"But if Flanagan's goal is to keep the stats low, I don't think she'd kill Rosenberg in the first place. I'm not great at math, but even I know that doesn't add up," I said.

"I think Flanagan is jealous of you and Wayne," Teeny said.

"How would jealousy of me and Wayne lead her to kill Rosenberg?" I asked. "Besides, there's no reason for her to be jealous."

"You're not kidding," Miss May said. "Does the guy even call anymore? One dance and he disappears like that sensual sashay never happened."

"That's a shame," Teeny said. "Detective Hudson is a big slice of hunkberry pie with sprinkles on top. You can't let that slip away, Chels!"

"Can we stop with all of this water fountain chatter?" I said. "This is serious business."

"Chelsea's right," Miss May said. "Let's focus on the case. Besides Teeny, I thought Big Dan was the only hunkberry pie you wanted to slice."

"Oh, stop," Teeny said. "Big Dan is a good-looking man. So what? Moving on. Are we sure Rosenberg's death wasn't part of a political conspiracy?"

"I don't think we can rule it out," I said. "Especially considering how close Chief Flanagan and Mayor Delgado have become. But the murder didn't feel planned out or conspiratorial. It felt up-close and personal. Unplanned."

"Agreed," Miss May said. "There were no signs of forced entry. So Rosenberg likely knew his killer. Plus, there are signs Rosenberg may have struggled with his assailants before being murdered."

"Or he had a fit and flipped the couch over himself," I said.

Miss May nodded. "Right. All that suggests the killing emerged from an argument or personal disagreement. Who have we learned might be the likely killer in that kind of scenario?"

"Lover?" I said. "Scorned spouse?"

"Russian secret agent with a thirst for violence that can't be quenched?" Teeny asked.

Miss May rolled her eyes.

Teeny shrugged. "What? That's just as likely as a scorned spouse."

"I think Chelsea may have gotten it right the first time," Miss May said. "We already mentioned Master Skinner's absence from the meeting. But someone else was absent, too. Someone who might have had even more motive to kill."

"Who?" I asked.

"Susan Rosenberg," Miss May said. "Hank's wife."

I nodded. "Oh yeah! It is weird she wasn't there."

"And then last night you two went by the Rosenberg house and no one was home, right?" Teeny asked.

Miss May nodded. "Yup."

Teeny hesitated. "I don't know though. Susan hosts some

pretty great cookie parties at the country club. She makes a divine Madeleine."

"So that means she can't be a killer?" Miss May asked.

"I don't know," Teeny said. "I like her cookies."

"Either way, we should probably go talk to Susan now, right?" I asked.

Miss May nodded. "We should offer our condolences. At least."

"Maybe we can bring her some pie." I said.

"Probably not," Miss May said. "Considering how Hank died."

I nodded. "Right. Facedown in pie. That would be insensitive."

Miss May stood and pulled her coat on. She let out a deep sigh and closed her eyes for a moment. It looked like she might faint.

I stood. "Miss May? Are you OK?"

"I'm fine." Miss May opened her eyes and looked at me. "I'm just getting ready. Are you ready?"

I nodded.

Miss May let out another deep exhale. "Here we go again."

11

OH DEAR, SUDEER

*M*iss May wanted to bring flowers to Susan instead of pie, so we stopped by Petunia's flower shop after breakfast to pick up a nice bouquet.

The walk down the hill to town was peaceful. But once we got back to Main Street we spotted a group of angry townspeople marching outside the Rosenberg Building.

Tom Gigley, the town lawyer, led the protestors. Behind him stood Brian, the owner of the *Brown Cow*. Brian's employees Rita and Willow brought up the rear along with Arthur, the owner of the gas station.

Although the group didn't quite manage to march or chant in unison, their faces were red and they shook their fists as they yelled.

Big Dan watched the spectacle from about 100 feet away.

Miss May crossed over to him. "What's going on here, Big Dan? Rosenberg is dead. Why is everyone still protesting?"

Big Dan had one eye on the crowd, and one eye on a vintage Indian motorcycle parked nearby.

"Rosenberg's people showed up this morning. Word is,

they're moving forward with the demolition." Big Dan pointed to the motorcycle. "Check out the paint job on that bike. That thing's probably older than I am, but it sure doesn't look it."

My designer's eye recognized that the motorcycle was indeed a masterwork of restoration. "Who owns it?"

"Arthur," Big Dan said. "He got it in a junkyard, spent years bringing it back to life. Did a great job, too."

Miss May shook her head. "I don't care about the bike, Big Dan! Why would they still be going through with the demolition?"

"Not sure," Big Dan turned to Miss May. "Oh by the way, I was thinking I might do apple fritters at *Big Dan's Donuts*. Is that OK with you? Don't want to steal your business or anything. You're the apple lady, so just say the word and I'll steer clear."

Miss May stood on her tippy-toes to get a better look at the protesters. "Sure, yeah. Fritters. No problem. Excuse me."

Miss May strode over to the protesters. I hung back for a second, and against my better judgment, leaned in to Big Dan and asked, "Big Dan, uh, what do you think of Teeny?"

Big Dan shrugged, "Well I did like that hashbrown lasagna she made." I waited for him to continue, but Big Dan wasn't a man of overflowing sentiment.

"OK," I said. And then before I could stop myself, I blurted, "She likes your beard!" Then I darted away and hurried toward Miss May.

As I neared the chanting crowd, I noticed Sudeer and a few contractors huddled near the entrance to the Rosenberg Building.

Miss May pushed her way through the crowd until she got to the front. "Sudeer. What's going on here? Your partner just died. That doesn't change anything? The Massive Mart is going forward as planned?"

Sudeer rubbed his temples, then looked up at Miss May. "We've delayed the demolition by a few days, out of respect."

"And you think it's smart to move forward with this Massive Mart?" Miss May asked. "Even after what happened to Rosenberg?"

"According to Chief Flanagan, he suffered a heart attack in his trailer. Are you saying something else might have happened?" Sudeer asked.

"I'm saying this town doesn't want this building!" Miss May said.

"Rosenberg's parent company wants to move forward. It's out of my hands." Sudeer checked the text on his phone and fired off a quick response.

I scratched my head. Parent company? What parent company? I took a step toward Sudeer.

"Can you stay off your phone while we talk?" Miss May asked. "This is important to people."

Arthur pushed his way up toward Miss May. "This guy doesn't care about anything but money, May. He's worse than Rosenberg!"

"I'm sorry. My little girl has a cold," Sudeer said. "That was a text for my wife."

"Wait, Sudeer...what parent company are you talking about?" I asked.

The chanting got louder. I repeated my question, but Sudeer couldn't hear me.

I yelled the question once more. Sudeer cupped his hand against his ear.

I was about to scream the question at the top of my lungs when Master Skinner emerged from his dojo.

"Quiet!"

Everyone at the protest stop yelling and turned.

Master Skinner was short and balding, with sharp brown eyes and a commanding presence. He was wearing his gi, fastened with his crisp black belt, as always. Even though I had just defended Master Skinner's gentle nature and kind soul, the echo of his deep voice settled in my chest like a rock.

"My students and I are deep in meditation. We are aligning our minds, bodies, and souls. Please. Be respectful."

Master Skinner cast a look across the crowd and the protestors shuffled away, many grumbling about how they were hungry for lunch anyway.

As I watched the protestors go, I wondered... *Could one of those people have killed Rosenberg?* Miss May and I needed to find out, or Sudeer might be the killer's next victim.

On the way over to Petunia's flower shop, Miss May called KP to see if he'd had any luck opening the briefcase. Judging by the look on her face, the prognosis was "not open."

"Not open?" I said.

"Not open now, not open ever," my aunt said. "KP said 'unless you can wake that Hankenstein fella from his eternal slumber' the case is impossible to open without destroying everything inside."

"It's not like KP to give up like that," I said. "Especially when it involves tearing something apart."

"Sounds like he tried every trick in the book," Miss May said. "Blow torch. Wrench. Crow bar. He didn't want to do more because he didn't want to risk damaging whatever's inside."

"That's thoughtful," I said, with a heavy sigh.

"Thoughtful and frustrating. But what can you do?"

As Miss May and I stepped into Petunia's, I couldn't help but smile, too. The little flower shop, barely bigger than a walk-in closet, brimmed with flowers. Bright red roses lined the back wall. Buttercups danced on the windowsill. And there was even an enormous teddy bear sitting on the counter, leftover from Valentine's Day.

Miss May smiled as she entered. For Miss May, a smile was better armor than a bulletproof vest. And she'd need it. The owner of the flower store, Petunia, was a notorious curmudgeon. When she wasn't at the flower shop she was running poker games at her retirement village. And she was five feet and one inch of fury, all wrapped up in a floral-print blouse.

Petunia glared as we entered. "May. What are you doing here?"

"Shopping for flowers," Miss May said. "What else?"

"Yeah I don't buy it," Petunia said.

"Well I hope you'll sell it," Miss May said. "I'll take an extra-large spring bouquet, please."

"Those bouquets are expensive. What do you want one for?"

Miss May's smile flickered. "Just taking flowers to a friend, Petunia."

Petunia narrowed her eyes. "Seems suspicious to me."

"Petunia. You sell flowers. I'm here to buy flowers. What's with the interrogation?"

"You know what? I'm right. I'm being rude. Pardon me for a second." Petunia turned around. I could have sworn she took a swig from a bottle before she turned back. "The stress is ruining my brain, that's all. Business is down from all this protesting. And I didn't have a good night at the poker tables. I'm being too aggressive. Too jumpy. It's because of this ridiculous Massive Mart. I'm telling you, that Rosenberg idiot will ruin our town from the grave!"

I looked over at Miss May. *Was it me or did Petunia sound a little defensive?*

Petunia groaned. "Don't exchange a conspiratorial glance with your aunt, Chelsea. Didn't we cover this last time? I'm not a killer."

"Sorry, Petunia," I said. "We're not here because we think you're a killer. We actually want to buy flowers."

"I don't believe you," Petunia said. "Sharing those suspicious looks. The two of you ought to be ashamed. My psychological wounds from the last time you questioned me are still festering and green. Now you prance into my store with more accusations?"

"Calm down, Petunia." Miss May took a step toward the counter. "We don't suspect you of anything. You're not even on our list of suspects."

"Did you say your wounds are festering and green? You might want to get that looked at," I said.

Petunia ignored me. "I wish I could trust you, May. But you weren't exactly forthright last time you questioned me."

Suddenly, Arthur exploded into the shop, shaking his fist. "Sudeer Patel is the biggest traitor this town has seen since—"

"We're all from Pine Grove, Arthur," Petunia said. "We know all about how Benedict Arnold spent a night in the church."

"Sudeer is worse than Benedict Arnold. That's what I'm trying to say. It smells wonderful in here, by the way. I love the bouquet of aromas you've cultivated in your place of business."

"As do I, Arthur," Miss May said. "Chelsea and I are actually here to buy flowers. But Petunia won't let us."

"I would let you buy flowers, if that's what you wanted," Petunia said. "But I know you're actually here to accuse me of killing that stupid, hideous Rosenberg."

"When you call him stupid and hideous, it doesn't exactly make you sound innocent," Miss May said. "However, I still don't suspect you. So can I have my flowers or not?"

"You should be ashamed, May," Arthur said. "Suspecting Petunia for this murder just like you suspected her of the last one? Just for having the gumption to oppose that money pig in public? It's preposterous. Ridiculous! Downright insulting."

Petunia handed Arthur a glass of water. "Here. Calm down. Have some water. Don't mind May and Chelsea. They're getting a little arrogant with all this sleuthing."

"Don't get me wrong," Arthur said. "I appreciate you catching those killers. Both of you. Hi Chelsea, by the way."

"Hi," I said.

"I'm just saying, when you start accusing townspeople, the people who make this little village great? That's when it starts to be too much. You've known Petunia how long? Thirty years? She's no killer."

"If there's one thing I've learned," Miss May said. "It's that anyone is capable of murder. Even those you least suspect."

"Listen to her with these grandiose quotations," Petunia said. "You know what, May. I resent that you're making me do this. But I don't need you snooping around my clubhouse, ruining anymore poker games. So here. I'll show you my alibi."

"You don't have to do that, Petunia," Miss May said. "We really don't think you did it."

"We don't," I insisted.

"No offense, Chelsea," Petunia said. "But hush your face."

Petunia pulled out her phone and opened up her photo album. "Here. See these pictures? I was at my granddaughter's birthday party the night Rosenberg died. We were playing CLUE. You know, the board game? Perhaps you should spend some more time playing that game. Could help you sharpen your detective skills. It was Mr. Green, in the library, with a candlestick. In case you were wondering."

"Ugh, it's always Mr. Green," I said. "Has anybody else noticed that? That guy is guilty every time!"

Petunia glared at me.

"Sorry. I shouldn't have said anything. Mr. Green is probably a gentleman. I don't suspect him for no reason. It's just, people named after colors kind of freak me out. Mustard? That's a color and a condiment! It gives me the chills."

"Are you done?" Petunia asked.

I nodded. "Yes. Sorry."

"Good." Petunia gestured for me to come closer. "Come take a look at this. OK?"

Petunia poked at her phone a couple times. "You poke here and you poke there. You can see where I was, geographically. And you can also see what time they took the photo. I took a class on computers last time you accused me, that way I could make sure I knew how to prove my innocence whenever necessary. Can't believe it's coming in handy so soon."

"We're not accusing you!" Miss May slammed her fist on the table. Petunia took a step back.

Miss May took a deep breath. "I'm sorry, Petunia. I honestly just wanted the flowers. That's it. I'm sorry I accused you last time. Whenever I question someone and turn out to be wrong... it haunts me. I regret that I made you feel like a suspect. And I should have apologized sooner."

A long silence hung in the air like particles of dust suspended in a beam of light. Finally, Petunia spoke, "You like lilies, right?"

Miss May cleared her throat and regained her composure. "Yes. They're my favorite."

Petunia went into the back room, and returned a few seconds later holding the biggest bouquet I had ever seen. There were so many flowers that Petunia was no longer visible behind them. And lilies were the most prominent ones. She handed the bouquet to Miss May.

"Extra lilies. Just for you."

Miss May accepted the bouquet. "Thanks. I hope your luck turns around at the tables."

"Poker is not a game of luck," Petunia said. "It's a game of skill. And I'll turn it around. Just as soon as these developers pick up and move to the next poor, unsuspecting town."

"Well said," Arthur replied.

Miss May looked from Arthur, then to Petunia, with a small smile. "You know, according to the police, Hank Rosenberg died of natural causes."

Petunia let out a small laugh. "We both know that's not true, May. Now go find the killer."

12

CASTLE CAPERS

$\mathcal{A}$s we approached Rosenberg's home, the imposing stone castle in the forest, I felt a warm unease in my stomach. The house was eerie in its enormity. And not a single light shone from inside.

That time, we knew Rosenberg wasn't going to be in. But it was almost 6 PM, so both Miss May and I thought his wife might be around.

Miss May handed me the bouquet and grabbed the big, brass knocker on the front door.

Clank. Clank. Clank.

No answer.

Clank. Clank. Clank.

Again, no answer.

"Here to offer your condolences?"

Miss May and I both yelped and spun around, flattening our backs against the door.

"I hear that's what you do when you question suspects," the disembodied voice continued. "Like a wolf in sheep's clothing."

We followed the sound of the voice and saw a middle-aged woman sitting on a bench about ten feet away, nestled in the golden twilight of the front yard.

She was tall, broad, and striking. Wearing all black with dramatic, smoky eyes. Her hair was pulled back in a simple, impeccable ponytail. And she had high cheek bones and pouty lips. *But not like from real pouting. Like, from a plastic surgeon.*

"Susan. We didn't see you there," Miss May said. "Chelsea. This is Susan Rosenberg, Hank's wife. Susan, this is Chelsea."

I nodded. "I'm sorry about your husband."

Susan stood from the bench and approached with her hands tucked behind her back. "I've been expecting the two of you. You often suspect the spouse in cases like these, no?"

There was a hint of a smirk on Susan's face, which chilled me.

"...uh." Miss May held out the bouquet. "We wanted to bring you these flowers. To say in person how sorry we are about what happened."

Susan turned back to the bench and ran a hand along the edge. "Hank and I bought this bench together. So we could enjoy nature. Drink fine wine. Watch the sunset."

"The sun sets in the opposite direction." I looked down as soon as I spoke. Why did I always have to correct people? Very annoying habit.

"It's a figure of speech, Chelsea." Susan's voice was sharp. "The point is: I wanted to enjoy our time together. And we did. Several times we sat on this bench. I cherish those moments now." Susan's eyes hardened. "Now that someone has killed Hank."

Miss May held up a finger. "According to the police—"

"Natural causes," Susan scoffed. "Stupid Sunshine Flanagan. That's ridiculous. Did you hear? Official cause of death, according to the police, was heart attack. Hank ran 6 miles every morning. His doctors said his heart was healthier than a thoroughbred racehorse. He did not have a heart attack."

Miss May nodded. She held out the flowers once more. "This bouquet has extra lilies. If you like them."

Susan offered Miss May a tight smile and accepted the flowers. "Lilies are beautiful. Thank you. But flowers are not what I want from you."

Miss May's eyebrows raised. "Oh?"

Susan shook her head. "I want you to find out who did this to my husband."

Miss May nodded. "We're going to do our best."

Susan crossed her arms. "Unbelievable. Can you imagine? One of these low-bred townie ingrates killed my thoroughbred."

Harsh, I thought. But I managed to keep silent.

"Hank started his career restoring old buildings, not demolishing them," Susan said. "Did you know that?"

Miss May and I shook our heads.

"When did he move on to megastores?" I asked.

Susan narrowed her eyes. "Hank doesn't just build megastores, silly. He restores entire towns. Restored them. Pine Grove is just one in a long line. My husband breathed new life into this entire region. Changed the socioeconomic makeup of the area, for the better. Did you know there's a term for that? It's called the Rosenberg Effect. A professor at Columbia coined the term a few years back. And it's real. People think big box stores ruin small towns. But they bring so much business, so many jobs. They raise so much money in taxes. The schools get better, the roads get better... Hence, the Rosenberg Effect."

I winced. Like most residents in Pine Grove, I was

against massive stores like the ones Hank Rosenberg built. Maybe Susan was right about the jobs and the influx of cash, but so what? Sometimes character was more important than profit. But again, I cautioned myself not to say anything. *Be still, my tongue.*

Miss May, on the other hand, didn't shy away from the conflict.

"You know most people hate those giant stores," she said.

"I'm well aware," Susan said. "Hence, the townie ingrates. The murder. Your investigation."

I looked over at Miss May. Susan was a staunch supporter of Rosenberg's work. She seemed bitter about his death. Not exactly signs that pointed to Susan's guilt. Miss May must have felt the same way, because she began to treat Susan more like a source of information, and less like a suspect.

"We want to solve the mystery of your husband's death," Miss May said. "But we need more information. Do you know anything that might be able to help?"

Susan smiled. "Oh yes. I know just where I'd start my investigation if I were you. Not everyone in this town is who they say they are. Some people have a secret past..."

Miss May took a step toward Susan. "Who are you referencing?"

Susan walked up the steps toward the front door. "Follow me and I'll show you."

As Susan led us through the house, I took a careful look around.

We entered into a small sitting room with floral wallpaper. A lush carpet gave way under my feet like fresh snow. Emily Dickinson novels lined a bookshelf on a far wall. In the corner, an easel propped up a half-finished painting of a hummingbird. And a daybed rested against the wall, with a worn copy of Shakespeare's Hamlet splayed out upon a pillow. *To build or not to build, that is the question...*

"I love this room," I said. "So delicate and thoughtful. I take it Hank didn't spend much time in here?"

Susan didn't break her stride as she rounded the corner into a hallway. "No. That's my room. For my painting and my reading. I didn't allow Hank in there."

Miss May and I exchanged a look as we followed Susan down the hall. *What did that mean?*

"Many couples live like that," Susan said. "Separate rooms for separate hobbies. Honestly, it was the secret to our marriage. Plenty of time apart."

We emerged at the end of the hallway into a room that I assumed was meant to be a formal dining room. But in the place of a dining table was a large billiards table. Images of old mobsters and classic movie posters decorated the lush, dark walls.

"Let me guess... Hank likes, er liked, to shoot pool?"

"He loved it. Tried to teach me, once. But I was a worse student of billiards than he was of oil painting. I put a hole in the wall with my cue stick during my first lesson and never played again."

Separate rooms for separate lives, I thought. *Isn't there something off about that?*

I looked over at Miss May. She craned her neck to get a look in another room, but Susan reached out and closed the door.

"Nothing in there. No need to snoop."

"Sorry," Miss May said. "I've got an energetic bladder. Thought that might be a powder room."

"I'll show you to the bathroom after," Susan said. "Come. Follow me."

With that, Susan walked toward a large oak door at the far end of an immaculate and spacious kitchen.

The door whined as Susan swung it open, then I heard her sensible heels thunk-thunk down a staircase.

Miss May and I paused at the top of the steps.

I whispered, "Are we really going to follow her down there?"

Miss May shrugged. "I think we've come too far to stay up here."

I looked down the steps. The walls of the staircase were stone, like the outside of the house. And whatever was down there had a misty, musty smell.

Susan reached the bottom of the staircase and turned back to us. "Come along. The basement won't bite. Well, not as long as you play nice."

Miss May descended the staircase. I followed, feeling like a frog was jumping up and down in my chest. The stairs spiraled downward in tight curves, and the light from the upstairs dimmed with each step I took.

Any second, a vampire could jump out and attack us, I thought. Or any other kind of basement horror. Nothing good ever lived in a basement. What if it was some sort of reptilian swamp monster with—

Whoa!

I missed the next step and stumbled down the final three to the bottom of the stairs. My arm shot out toward the wall to steady me, and I recoiled at the coldness of the stone. My body tingled with goosebumps.

Did it just get ten degrees colder, or am I crazy?

I gathered myself and looked around the basement.

And I couldn't believe what I saw.

13

TROPHY WIFE

*R*osenberg's basement was not the den of horrors I had expected.

In fact, it was the most pristine basement I had ever seen. Presumably expensive bottles of red wine lined the far wall. A 60-inch TV hung opposite a burgundy leather couch. And an enormous trophy case occupied the back wall.

I had envisioned the basement filled with human bones or ancient torture equipment. Somehow this elegant trophy room creeped me out even more.

The whole place had an antiseptic feel. Like if a dentist's office had a big screen TV. And expensive furniture.

"Wow. This is a wonderful man cave," I said.

Susan tittered. "Man cave? This is a man sanctuary. To Hank, it was a holy place. Even I find solace here. The enormity of the television humbles me."

I shot a look at Miss May. Was it me or did Susan Rosenberg sounds like a bonafide maniac?

I sat on the couch and let out a moan of comfort. That was the most comfortable couch I had ever experienced.

Despite the circumstances, I wanted to curl up on it and take a nap.

"I didn't bring you down here just so you could moan on my dead husband's exquisite couch," Susan said.

"Right," I said, standing up. "Sorry. The couch called my name. That is an incredible piece of furniture. I would... marry that couch. And we would have a rich and vibrant relationship. Just me and the couch against the world. Me and Couchy."

"That's good, Chelsea," Miss May said. "You can stop talking."

I nodded. My nervous chatter was making everyone uncomfortable, including me.

Susan gestured to the trophy case along the back wall. "Look here and tell me what you see."

I saw five long shelves stacked with golden trophies. There were also a few plaques and framed newspaper clippings among the awards. The centerpiece was a big picture of Hank, holding one of the trophies above his head.

"A challenge," Miss May said. "I like it. What do you think, Chelsea? See any clues in the trophy case?"

Miss May stood back to get a good overview. I wanted to get a closer look, so I approached the largest trophy and read the inscription.

"Hank Rosenberg, State Champion, Karate. 1980."

I turned back to Susan and Miss May. "Hank was a karate champion?"

Susan nodded. "Hank was a karate master. The best this area has ever seen."

I looked back at Susan. The best? I'd always assumed...

Miss May didn't beat around the tush. Or the bush. She got straight to it. "So you're trying to tell us Master Skinner was involved in the murder."

"Keep looking," Susan said. "I'm also providing you his motive."

"Master Skinner's dojo is in the Rosenberg Building," I said. "The demolition of his livelihood wasn't his motive?"

Susan shook her head. "Oh no. The motive was very much karate-related, young lady. I'm telling you: behind Master Skinner's zen exterior, there lurks the soul of a sour fruit."

Miss May looked skeptical. She narrowed her eyes and turned back to the trophy case. As did I.

I inspected one trophy after another. Each had been inscribed with Hank's name. And the years spanned from the 1970's into the 1980's.

"All this is telling me is that Hank was great at karate," I said to Miss May. "That's surprising, sure. But so what?"

"I'm not sure," Miss May said. "We need to find the connection."

"My husband was born and raised in Pine Grove," Susan volunteered. "His family lived here for generations. Some say you can feel their spirits in the walls."

I forced a smile but felt terrified inside. *OK, creepy lady. Keep your distance.*

I turned to Miss May. "Maybe Master Skinner and Rosenberg were high school rivals on the karate circuit," I said. "Perhaps Master Skinner was evening an old score? Could that be the theory?"

Miss May shook her head. "Master Skinner is at least five or ten years younger than Rosenberg. They weren't at PGHS at the same time. They wouldn't have been rivals."

"Interesting observation," Susan said. "But they both may have pursued karate competitively beyond high school."

I sighed. I felt like if Susan had information that could

help our investigation, she should spit it out already. I was about to give Susan more than just a piece of my mind when Miss May perked up.

"Wait!" Miss May turned to Susan. "There was that big regional karate tournament! In the mid-eighties, it was all anyone talked about for a few weeks. I remember, because two of the contestants were from Pine Grove."

Susan nodded.

Miss May continued. "Master Skinner was one of the finalists."

Susan stood tall. "And the other was my husband."

Miss May nodded. "I had forgotten about that tournament, but it was a big deal." My aunt turned to me and explained. "They called it the 'Foot-Fist-Fight-a-thon.' It wasn't an official competition. I think it was for charity. But the winners got big-time bragging rights. Everybody thought Pine Grove's young, rising star would win."

"Master Skinner?" I asked.

Miss May nodded.

"And he was fighting Rosenberg?" I asked.

Susan looked into the distance. "Hank was in his twenties then. It was the end of his prime."

"That's right!" Miss May covered her mouth. "I remember that. It's all coming back to me. Everyone thought Master Skinner was unbeatable. People called him 'Skinner the Winner' for months before the tournament took place."

Susan nodded. "It was inconceivable that he might lose."

"But did he lose?" I asked.

"The way I heard it," Miss May started, side-eyeing Susan for confirmation, "Master Skinner let the hype go to his head. He spent too much time giving interviews. He even appeared in a commercial for a local car dealership. So then when the match finally took place—"

"Skinner was weak," Susan said. "Undisciplined. Out of practice."

"And?" I asked.

Susan grinned. "Hank defeated his opponent handily. And footily."

"Whoa. So Rosenberg beat Skinner in the biggest tournament of the 80s." I turned to Miss May. "But Master Skinner wouldn't have killed Hank because of a decades-old charity tournament."

"Sure he would have," Susan said. "You know how they say those who can't do, teach?"

"I've always thought that was a fallacy that unfairly demeans teachers," I said. *Darn it, tongue, didn't I tell you to be still?*

"Well in Master Skinner's case, it's the truth," Susan retorted, with an edge in her voice. "He abandoned his career as a karate champion after the charity tournament. Opened his practice a few months later. Never competed again."

"So Hank ruined Master Skinner's life," Miss May said.

"No!" Susan bellowed and swiped a few of Hank's trophies off the shelf. They clattered on the floor and echoed in the man cave.

Miss May and I took a step back, stunned by Susan's outburst.

Susan turned on Miss May, glaring. "Skinner's dojo only thrived thanks to my husband's affordable rental rates. Hank was a blacker belt than Skinner. That's all! Skinner couldn't admit it."

Miss May held up her hands in surrender. "You're right. I hyperbolized. I'm sorry."

"Master Skinner always blamed Hank for the way things turned out, but hubris was that little man's undoing."

My eyes widened. "Wow. Master Skinner always seemed humble to me. Exceedingly humble, in fact."

Susan guffawed. "Oh, he turned it around. 'Rebranded' himself as a 'zen messiah.' But don't be a fool. Master Skinner has let his grudge against my husband boil his blood for years. Years!"

"But I don't understand," I said. "If Master Skinner hated your husband so much, why did he rent his dojo from Hank in the first place?"

Miss May shook her head. "You don't remember. That building hasn't always been the Rosenberg building. Hank purchased it and renamed it after Master Skinner moved in."

"But kept the rates low! Out of generosity!" Susan reminded us.

"Still, I find it hard to believe that a man with such, er, hubris as Master Skinner would deign to rent anything from his sworn nemesis." I was trying to tread lightly. Susan seemed prone to taking things personally.

"Not a lot of empty storefronts in town. Not sure he had much choice." Miss May turned to Susan. "Is that what this Massive Mart location was really about? Was it just part of Rosenberg's plan to spite Master Skinner?"

Susan shrugged. "At the least, it was a pleasing side effect. But Hank... He never thought... Neither of us expected Master Skinner to, to kill."

Susan looked down. She sniffled and wiped a tear away. When she looked up, her eyes were flinty and set. "Get him. Please. The police won't help me. And I need you to put that man away for life."

That night, Teeny called the bakeshop and placed an order for a few dozen cinnamon buns, "Chelsea-style."

Apparently, Miss May had told Teeny all about my cinnamon buns and the secret ingredient, and Teeny wanted to sell some at *Grandma's* that weekend.

Teeny's order flattered me. But it also grumped me up a little. Neither Miss May nor I felt like engaging in a marathon baking session after talking to Susan Rosenberg, but we liked to fill Teeny's orders quickly, so we got right to work.

As soon as we began to knead the dough, Liz walked through the door of the bakeshop.

"Wow. It smells amazing in here. What are you two baking?"

Miss May laughed. "We haven't put anything in the oven yet. So unless you love the smell of instant yeast, you're flattering us because you want something."

Liz took out a reporter's notebook from her back pocket. "OK. You got me. I'm here for a quote on a story I'm reporting."

"We're not going to comment on an ongoing investigation," Miss May said.

"I'm not here about any investigations," Liz said. "I'm wondering if you know any eligible tomcats for Sandra Day O'Connor. We're running a two page spread on her search for love and I want to add quotes from local residents. Give it the depth that people expect from me."

"Is it that hard to find a single cat in Pine Grove?" Miss May asked. "I see three or four new strays a week."

"Agreed," I said. "If only it were that easy to find actual bachelors in Pine Grove, it would solve a lot of problems for me."

"Does that mean things are cooling off between you and Wayne Hudson?" Liz asked.

I slapped my head with my palm. "I was making a joke. I don't want to talk about that."

"So then there is something to talk about? Tell me about this slow dance. Were Wayne's hands over your shoulders or around your waist? And where does Germany Turtle fit into this love triangle? I hear he's hot for Chelsea, too."

"From whom!?" I asked.

"From him," Liz said. "He proclaims his love for you to everyone he meets."

My face flushed red. "Well I'm single."

Liz pulled out a recorder and held it to my mouth. "And ready to mingle?"

"I thought you were here to talk about cats." I angled my face away from the recorder.

"That's just her decoy story," Miss May said. "She's still after news on our investigation. Isn't that right, Liz?"

"No," Liz said. "That's crazy! I wouldn't lie to you. I heard you were talking to Susan Rosenberg, that's all. Are you sure you're not baking something that smells delicious? Maybe I'm just smelling residual deliciousness from another day."

"Where did you hear that?" Miss May asked.

"I didn't. But thank you for confirming it." Liz made a quick note on her pad. "So Master Skinner must be suspect number one then. I'm presuming you and Susan discussed what happened in the Foot-Fist Fight-a-thon those many years ago?"

"No comment, Elizabeth. And I'm serious. Please don't run any stories about this. Not yet. It could ruin the entire investigation."

Liz narrowed her eyes. Looked between me and Miss May. "Fine. I'll keep a lid on the story. For now. But I'm a good resource. Remember how great I was at the library last time?"

"You were great," Miss May said. "And you're right. You are a resource. What do you think about the whole Master Skinner thing?"

"I think he has motive, that's for sure," Liz said. "Did it look like Rosenberg might have been karate chopped to death?"

Miss May sighed. "I'm not sure exactly what that might look like. But it's possible."

Liz nodded. "That makes me sad. I like Skinner. He's spunky."

"We like him too," Miss May said. "But justice requires us to pursue the truth. So tomorrow morning... That's exactly what we're going to do."

"And you don't know any cats for Sandra Day O'Connor?"

Miss May shook her head. "I'll put out some tuna tonight. See if we can attract an eligible bachelor."

14

LITTLE KIMMY ATTACKS

*T*he next morning, we woke up and went straight to Master Skinner's dojo to question Skinner in person.

We were about halfway through the parking lot when Big Dan slid out from under a pickup truck with a smile on his face and a wrench in his hand.

"Morning ladies! How are you two doing today? I'm grrreat!" He said 'great' with a growl, just like Tony the Tiger.

Miss May laughed. "We're doing well, how are you Big Dan? Whoops! You already told us."

"Yup! I'm grrrreat." Big Dan stood up and wiped his hands on his jeans. "I got my 10,000 steps in before 6 AM so I'm not going to walk a single step for the rest of the day."

Miss May nodded in appreciation. "Wow. I didn't even know Pine Grove had 10,000 steps. Teeny always says the cops just walk in circles in the park to get their exercise."

Big Dan took a big sip of water. "Oh yeah, I went in circles. Heh. That Teeny's kinda funny, huh?"

Miss May and I exchanged glances.

"Hilarious," I agreed. "She is a bundle of wit and charm."

Big Dan smiled. "Hey. How are your cars doing? All good? Need a tuneup? Checkup? Top off your fluids, free of charge? You know that big old German bus burns oil, May. And that pickup is no spring chicken, Chelsea. More like an October chicken if you ask me."

"We're all good, thanks," Miss May said. "Although when you switch over to donuts, I'll be a frequent customer."

"Who knows when that'll happen," Big Dan said. "Donuts are a tricky business. You have a good day now!"

Miss May laughed as we walked toward the dojo. "You too, Big Dan."

I looked back and narrowed my eyes at Big Dan. "That guy is nice. A little too nice?"

"I think just regular nice," Miss May said. "Not a suspect."

"I think he might be a suspect in Teeny's romantic life."

"OK, Chels," Miss May said. "Now's not the time for matchmaking."

"Sorry." #NotSorry.

We arrived at the front door to Skinner's dojo and Miss May turned to me. "You feeling good? Ready for this?"

I shrugged. "I'm grrrreat."

Inside Master Skinner's dojo, the vibe was studious and serious. Three rows of stone-faced children grunted and karate chopped in unison. Master Skinner guided the students at the front of the room. But the weirdest thing was by far the tall, strange man practicing along with the kids in the back row.

It was Germany Turtle.

Germany was a step behind all the other kids and sweating twice as much.

Miss May nudged me. "Look who it is."

"Will you shush?" I said. "I'm looking for clues."

Miss May giggled, and we looked around. The dojo hadn't changed much since I had taken lessons there as a kid. It felt familiar yet fresh, as if it had recently gotten a makeover. Or a facelift. Or both. Soft blue mats lined the floors. And inspirational posters dotted the walls every few feet.

"Inner peace is outer power."

"Think your way to victory."

"Your greatest opponent is yourself."

None of the slogans seemed to suggest murdering your enemies. Still, Master Skinner had an intense energy as he instructed the students. I wondered, *could he be the killer?*

Thirty seconds after we entered, Master Skinner turned his intense focus on me and Miss May.

"Chelsea Thomas. A former champion from this very dojo. Welcome."

I smiled, nervous. "Hi, Master Skinner. Funny seeing you here."

Master Skinner turned to the class. "Students, it is my pleasure to introduce you to Chelsea Thomas. She hides behind humor but inside has an unfathomable strength. Come, Chelsea. Join me for a demonstration."

I blushed. "I haven't practiced karate in years. You'd be better off using one of these kids."

"Nonsense," Master Skinner said. "I've read in the Pine Grove Gazette you use karate to apprehend killers in your mystery investigations."

"Master's right," Germany Turtle said. "I read those articles, too. You're great at karate, Chelsea. And you do have a strength unfathomable."

I demurred and stumbled back toward the entrance. But then Germany began chanting my name, and the students joined in.

"Chel-sea! Chel-sea! Chel-sea!"

Miss May leaned in and whispered. "I think you better get out there, Chelsea. Or we'll have a riot on our hands."

I looked from the students, to Germany, then back to Master Skinner. I gulped and tried to muster a smile. "OK. What are we demonstrating?"

Moments later, I stood in the center of the mat beside a 10-year-old girl named "Little Kimmy."

"Kimmy will attack. Chelsea will demonstrate the uke, then the otoshi uke. And she will utilize the morote uke, if necessary. Do you remember those terms?"

"Uh... Block? And forearm block? Something like that?"

"Terrific," Master Skinner said. "It will all come back to you, I'm sure. And...begin!"

As soon as the fight began, I clammed up. Literally, every inch of my skin turned clammy. Little Kimmy looked ripped for a 10-year-old, and she circled me like a predator circles a scared little mouse.

At first she came at me slowly, with a standard kick. My sense memory kicked in and I managed a block.

I looked over at Miss May. She smiled and flashed a thumbs-up.

Little Kimmy launched another kick-attack. Once again, I managed a block.

Germany stood and pumped his fist. "Yeah! Get that small child, Chelsea!"

Seconds after Germany stood, the other students took to

their feet as well. Unlike Germany, however, the other students rooted for Little Kimmy, not me.

"Go Little Kimmy!"

"Take her down, Little Kimmy!"

"She's soft in the middle! Hit her there!"

The more the kids cried out, the more Germany defended me. "Hey!" he said. "That's no way to talk to a lady!"

But the children were louder than Germany, and his singular voice was no match for their enthusiasm.

As the chanting grew louder, Little Kimmy attacked with increased ferocity. I gave up on blocking her hits and decided instead to employ evasive maneuvers. But the more I attempted to dodge Little Kimmy's hits, the more disoriented I became.

Then, in one fluid motion, Little Kimmy kicked my feet out from under me and pinned me to the mat. *Well, this is humiliating,* I thought. *Hopefully she won't notice how clammy I am.*

Little Kimmy kept me pinned for a few seconds, smiling in my face, then she jumped up with a smile and cheered in victory.

"I did it! I won! She's so sweaty! But like, also cold." *Gee thanks, Kimmy.*

Master Skinner approached and helped me up. "Chelsea. You have always made that mistake. You lose balance trying to avoid being hit. But what have I always told you?"

"To lean in?" I winced, suddenly aching everywhere. "You didn't want me to demonstrate defensive tactics at all, did you? You wanted to teach me a lesson."

"I got what I wanted," Master Skinner said. "All I want is for you to do the same."

When I turned back from the water fountain, Germany Turtle was standing right behind me. "Chelsea. It was my divine pleasure to see you fight this morning. Little Kimmy is a cheater. You deserve to win."

"I was trying to demonstrate defense," I said. "And I failed . But thank you, I guess."

"Have you thought about me since we last saw one another and I professed my interest in your wondrous mind and curvaceous physical form?"

I looked around. *Whewph*. No one was within earshot. "Not really, Germany. I've kind of been investigating this murder."

Germany nodded. "I assume you speak of Hank Rosenberg's so-called heart attack?"

Shoot! Way to blab, Chels.

"I'm glad you're pursuing the truth," Germany said. "Applying the same brilliant thinking you used to solve my parents' case to another poor, slaughtered soul. You are a selfless and beautiful creature, Chelsea Thomas. Can I take you to the movies?"

Woof, this guy was forward! Fast forward!

I, on the other hand was slow. "Uhhhh...."

"I'm sorry, was that untoward? It's just, I read on varied Internet sites that people in small-town America accompany one another to the cinema as the first step on their romantic journeys. Is that incorrect?"

"No," I said. "That's correct. But hold on a second... Have you never gone to the movies with someone before?"

"My parents forbade me from attending movie theaters. They insisted I only see Broadway musicals. And even then, they permitted me only to see those works which had music and lyrics by Sondheim."

I stammered. "Wow. That's intense, Germany. Have you seen any movies?"

Germany laughed. "Oh yes, I've seen movies. I've seen several World War II documentaries. And I've seen every cinematic reproduction of Shakespeare's tragedies. Those were real popcorn flicks, as they say. Anyway, take some time to consider. We can go as platonic acquaintances, no need to call it a date."

Miss May approached and took me by the elbow. "Chelsea. Can I grab you for a moment? I think Master Skinner is about to teach a new class."

I looked back at the dojo. Master Skinner straightened the floor-mats along the wall.

"Sure." I said. "Nice to see you, Germany. You need to watch a real movie, at some point."

"Name your favorite and I'll buy ten copies," Germany said.

"Why would you..." I trailed off. Germany's sincerity charmed me. "OK. I'll think about it."

Miss May and I waited for Germany to exit, then we hovered as Master Skinner continued to straighten the mats for his next class.

He addressed us without looking up from the mats. "Is there something I can help the two of you with?"

Miss May nodded. "There is something you can help us with. Yes."

Master Skinner stood and gave us a small bow. "Please. Speak quickly. For you, I am a setting sun."

"What does that mean?" Miss May said.

"In moments I will be dark. For I will have a new mountain of minds to mold."

Miss May nodded. "Oh. I get it. Cool."

Master Skinner narrowed his eyes. "Cool? Is that a word in your vocabulary now?"

Miss May shrugged. "I don't know. You said the setting sun thing. So I blathered. We're here to talk about Rosenberg."

Master Skinner turned away. He pressed his palms together in a prayer pose. "What about him?"

"Well... We're trying to gather information about his death. He was your landlord. Did you know him well?"

"I paid the rent online. I doubt we met more than a handful of times."

I looked over at Miss May. Master Skinner was lying. *Why?*

"And how did you feel about the demolition of the Rosenberg building? You've had your dojo here for decades. It's hallowed ground."

"Rosenberg's plans for demolition did not bother me. I intended to retire to Orlando later this year."

Wait, what?!

"That makes little sense," Miss May said. "These mats you're arranging are brand-new. I also noticed three new air-conditioning units outside the dojo. And are those new hardwood floors beneath the mats?"

I looked around. The dojo had seemed so similar to me. But Miss May was right on all counts. Master Skinner had poured a lot of money into the place and it looked like he had done so in the past few months.

"OK. My plans to retire emerged after I learned of the demolition. I loved teaching in this building. I can't imagine doing so anywhere else. Other than Orlando."

"Why Orlando?" I asked.

Master Skinner looked confused, like, "Why not Orlando?"

I continued. "I'm just saying... Central Florida is hot all the time. And you're not even near the beaches. I'm sorry. But like, do you love Disney? Do you enjoy unrelenting humidity? I should stop talking. I'm going to stop talking."

"Look, Master Skinner," Miss May said. "I'm just going to come out with this. Because I respect you. Did you kill this guy?"

Master Skinner blanched. "What? No. Why would you think that?"

"We know about the Foot-Fist Fight-a-thon for charity. You said you had only met Rosenberg once or twice but the two of you have a deep history. He defeated you in battle. Why did you lie?"

"Because I don't like talking about that time in my life," Master Skinner said. "I could have been a karate champion. But Hank Rosenberg's victory derailed my plans and damaged my vulnerable young ego. I gave up the competition circuit and worked at *Pizza Plus* to earn enough to open my dojo. It is a fine life, but not the life I might have had, in another dimension."

"I love *Pizza Plus*," I clapped my hands over my mouth. "Sorry. That was an insensitive response to the very profound thing you said."

"It's fine," Master Skinner said. "Their crust was delicious, but I always thought the sauce was too bitter."

"So you had the motive," Miss May prodded. "The man banished you to a life of mediocre pizza-making."

Master Skinner nodded. "I'll admit. I've fantasized about hurting Rosenberg. I have the skills. But that's not what karate is about. I teach my students to achieve prosperity through peace. And that's how I live my life. At least this life, in this dimension."

Miss May turned and looked at the slogans on the wall.

"You weren't at the town hall meeting the night Rosenberg died. Where were you?"

"You need an alibi?" Master Skinner asked.

"She's just being thorough," I said. "As you would be."

"Fine. I was on a date." Master Skinner looked away, embarrassed.

"OK," Miss May said. "Thank you. Can you tell us who you were with?"

Master Skinner shook his head. "Technically I was supervising a date."

Miss May and I exchanged a confused look.

Master Skinner threw up his hands, exasperated. "I brought my cat to go meet Deb's cat, OK? Sandra Day O'Connor is looking for a mate and I thought she might get along with my kitty Bruce Lee."

"But Deb made her announcement about Sandra at the town hall meeting," I said. "How did you..."

"I have also been actively looking for a life partner for Bruce, alright?" Skinner said, sounding more defensive than he had when we'd accused him of murder. "Deb said I could make the introduction while she was at the meeting. Apparently, Deb likes to give her cat 'purring room' when Sandra meets new people."

Miss May stifled a laugh. "I take it things didn't go well?"

"Apparently Bruce Lee is not a good enough listener for Sandra Day O'Connor. That's ridiculous! She yowled for a full hour and he sat there the whole time, licking his paw."

"Love is a difficult thing," Miss May said. "Thank you for talking to us."

"Please," Master Skinner said. "Tell no one. Bruce Lee has a delicate ego." *Like his owner, I guess.*

Miss May locked her lips with an imaginary key. She

handed me the key, and I did the same. Then I ate the key. Then I realized, eating the key with my locked lips created a problematic paradox. I sighed. Life can be so complicated.

"Thank you for your discretion," Master Skinner said. "And Chelsea. Remember. Lean in. In karate and in life."

15

LUNCHES AND HUNCHES

*T*eeny swallowed an enormous bite of cinnamon bun and chased it with a glug of coffee. "That's ridiculous. Bruce Lee would never be a good match for Sandra Day O'Connor!"

Miss May laughed. "I don't know either feline well enough to say."

"I do," Teeny said. "Sandra Day O'Connor is a special cat. Beautiful, of course. But particular. And Bruce Lee? That tomcat is so full of himself, he thinks his kitty litter don't stink. Like I said. Not a good match."

I laughed. "I like that you have such strong opinions about these things."

"They're not opinions," Teeny said. "They're facts."

"OK. We've discussed the cats enough." Miss May sipped her coffee. "I thought you'd be more interested in the case, to be honest."

"You know I'm interested in the case," Teeny said. "Master Skinner is innocent. So where do we go from here?"

I took a big bite of cinnamon bun. The frosting smushed on my nose and I tried to reach up with my tongue and lick it off. That's what a classy lady would do, right? Still chewing, I said, "We never got an alibi from Rosenberg's wife."

"That's true," Miss May said. "She redirected us to the trophy case and kept the attention off herself. We got so distracted we never got around to her alibi."

"She was cagey," I said. "And that castle-mansion gave me the heebie-jeebies."

Teeny leaned in. "How are you spelling heebie-jeebies?"

"Uh, I don't know, I guess, H-E-E-B-I-E dash J-E-E-B-I-E-S?"

"Huh. No Y. Interesting." Teeny took a bite of cinnamon bun. "I would have used a Y."

Miss May rolled her eyes. "As fascinating as this conversation is, Chelsea's right. Rosenberg's home had an unsettling air."

"Like... Susan and Hank had separate rooms for everything," I explained to Teeny. "There was a reading room for her. Billiards room for him."

Teeny waved me off. "So what? Ample alone time is the secret to a strong marriage."

Miss May poured herself more coffee. "Teeny's right."

"You're both single!" I said.

"I was married. A few times," Teeny said. "It never worked out."

"Not enough alone time?" I asked.

"Well, I always did get along better with my husbands after the divorce."

Miss May nodded in affirmation. "She did."

How romantic...

"Besides, Susan doesn't fit the scene of the crime," Miss May said. "Remember... the killer was on foot. He or she escaped out the back. And the assailant scuffled with Hank before killing him."

"So what?" I asked. "Susan is thin enough to have slipped out that back window. And if it were her, she would not have needed to force entry into the trailer. That fits the profile for the killer, too. And she seemed like she might have crazy adrenaline strength."

Miss May shook her head. "Point is, Susan had thousands of opportunities to kill Hank. And she is such a meticulous person. Why would she have murdered her husband in such a sloppy way?"

"Plus, neither of you have any idea what Susan's motive might be. Other than that she was Rosenberg's wife." Teeny took another bite of cinnamon bun.

"That's true," I said. "But then who do we question next?"

Teeny smiled her devious smile and rubbed her hands together. "I've got a theory."

"Please don't tell us about some episode from the *North Port Diaries*," Miss May said.

"Hear me out, would you?" Teeny laid her hands flat on the table. "Yes. This theory is from *North Port Diaries*. But I think it's a good one... What if the mayor was being bribed by Rosenberg? Rosenberg might have been controlling Delgado with money. Forcing her to support a project she would otherwise hate. What if, after months of abuse, the mayor got sick of being under Rosenberg's dirty little thumb, so she killed him for her freedom?"

Teeny sat back and turned her hands up like she had just performed a magic trick. "Now that's what I call a theory. With sprinkles on top. What do you girls think?"

Miss May looked at me. I shrugged. I had heard crazier ideas. From Teeny. In the past week.

Miss May looked back at Teeny. "Honestly?"

Teeny leaned in, excited.

"It's the best theory we've got," Miss May said. "So let's go talk to the mayor."

Pine Grove's Town Hall was a two-story brick building set two blocks off Main Street. There was a small lawn, a parking lot in back, and a sign posted out front that said: "Pine Grove Town Hall."

On that day, Wallace the Traveler paced in front of the sign, screaming at the top of his lungs. "We want a pitcher not a belly itcher!"

Miss May slowed her step as we approached from the parking lot. "Poor guy. Should we give him a few bucks?"

Wallace punched the air and screamed, "Come on, ump! What kind of call is that? Go suck a sewer!"

"It sounds like he's at a baseball game," I said. "And his team is not winning."

"Good point," Miss May said, "we'll catch him next time."

We hurried up the steps to Town Hall as Wallace continued to yell. But once we slipped inside, the sound disappeared, and the quiet of the building absorbed us.

Upon entering, a simple sign greeted us, "Press Conference Upstairs."

Miss May shrugged and followed the sign up to a meeting hall on the second floor. There we found Mayor Linda Delgado speaking at a podium.

There were several rows of chairs set up in front of the podium, but Liz was the only person in the audience. And she took diligent notes in her pad as the mayor spoke.

Miss May and I slipped inside and stood along the back wall to watch.

The mayor said a few kind words about Hank Rosenberg and mentioned that her thoughts were with his family.

Beyond that, her speech indicated that everything in Pine Grove was business as usual.

The mayor emphasized that the Massive Mart would still be built in Pine Grove, despite Rosenberg's death, and confirmed that the demolition of the Rosenberg Building would begin on Monday. She claimed that Pine Grove needed an influx of business and argued that the towns-people should be grateful any business would build in town after so many murders. After fifteen solid minutes, she opened the floor to questions.

Both Liz and Miss May shot their hands up.

The mayor smiled down from her podium. "Liz, Miss May, nice to see you both. I'm sorry, May. I'm only taking questions from those with press badges this afternoon."

Miss May groaned. "That means you're only taking questions from Liz. Pine Grove only has one newspaper. We have no television stations. We only have one member of the press."

The mayor offered a tight smile. "I don't make the rules. But I do enforce them."

You also make them, I thought.

Liz stretched her hand into the air like an eager elementary school student.

The mayor pointed at Liz. "Liz. Question?"

Liz stood and spoke. "Yes. It seems everyone but you hates the idea of a Massive Mart in Pine Grove. How do you think your support of this initiative will affect your next campaign?"

"The people of this fine town elected me to represent their needs, not their wants. It's difficult for me to turn away from my constituents when they oppose what I think is right. But as their representative, it is my duty to do so."

Miss May scoffed. "Yeah, right."

"No comments unless you're a member of the press," Mayor Delgado said. "Thank you so much. Anything else, Liz?"

Liz asked the mayor for a detailed financial breakdown of the economic benefits that the Massive Mart would have on Pine Grove. The mayor launched into a long-winded answer and Miss May and I slid into the seat next to Liz.

Miss May nudged Liz's elbow. "Psst. Liz."

Liz didn't take her eyes off the mayor. "What's up, Miss May?"

"Will you ask some of my questions? I'll give you free pie for life."

Liz shook her head. "I'm a proud member of the press. You can't bribe me with pie. That said, I'm willing to ask your questions if they're good."

Miss May leaned in and whispered her questions. Liz jotted the questions down, nodding or making the occasional comment as she listened.

The next time the floor was open for questions Liz shot her hand back up.

"Expansion. Growth. Big business. These have never been the fundamental tenets of your role as mayor of this town. You've always been a small-town mayor. You supported the festivals and the farmers market. You supported the people. Yes, you were in favor of installing traffic lights, but that is a far cry from supporting a monstrosity such as the Massive Mart. Can you explain this change of heart?"

The mayor sighed. "Do we have to do this, Liz? It's early. I haven't even finished my coffee from breakfast."

"Please answer the question," Liz said. "Unless you'd rather I report you're an enemy of the press."

Miss May laughed. She loved Liz's tenacity and so did I.

"Okay," the mayor said. "Can you repeat the question?"

"How about I ask a different question, mayor? And I'll be blunt so you can understand. Are you being blackmailed or bribed by Hank Rosenberg's parent company to support the Massive Mart in Pine Grove? That's the only way I can explain your behavior."

Delgado blinked, stunned. "How dare you insult me like that at my press conference! One more inappropriate question and I will revoke your press badge."

"You can't do that!" Liz stood on her chair and thrust her fist into the air. "Freedom of the Press! Freedom of the Press!"

The mayor turned beet red. "Elizabeth! Get off your chair. I'll call your mother right now!"

"Go ahead," Liz said. "Call my mom! She hates this Massive Mart just as much as everybody else. If you get her on the phone, tell her I said hi!"

The mayor gathered her papers and walked off the stage. "This press conference is over!"

The mayor slammed the door as she exited. My jaw dropped as I listened to her heels clack down the hall.

Then Liz climbed off her chair with a smile. "I think that went well, don't you?"

16

BAKIN' BREAK-IN

*W*hen Miss May and I emerged from Town Hall, perfect summer weather greeted us like a puppy after a long day at work. It was 80 degrees. The air was warm and moist. And a light breeze kept things cool. It was, by all accounts, a beautiful summer day. Not counting the murder, of course.

"That was some press conference," Miss May said.

I chuckled. "Sure was. A lot we need to discuss."

Miss May side-eyed me. "What are you thinking?"

"I'm thinking it's a warm summer day. Maybe a cold, creamy treat might get our brain juices flowing."

Miss May broke into a wide smile. "Cohen's Cones or the Big Pig?"

"Only the two most legendary ice cream shops in the tri-state area," I said. "How lucky is it that they both happen to be in Pine Grove?"

"Lucky. So? What do you think?"

I looked up into the sky and thought about it. "Well... Those big puffy clouds put me in the mood for a giant scoops from the Big Pig. But I'm craving soft-serve."

Miss May headed down Main Street on foot. "Let's walk. By the time we get there, we'll have burned enough calories to get two scoops instead of one."

I laughed. That wasn't true, but I leaned in. "Or three scoops instead of two."

Miss May laughed. "That's my girl."

Cohen's Cones was housed in a little white shack about a five-minute walk from the center of town. The spot was popular because it was right off the Pine Grove bike trail. And because the proprietor, Sam Cohen, served the creamiest, softest ice cream in the world.

Sam smiled big as we approached. He was in his sixties, with curly salt and pepper hair. And he had a space between his front teeth just wide enough to fit a Tic-Tac. "The Thomas sisters! I don't officially consider it summer until I see your smiling faces. You're a little late this year, but I'm thrilled to announce the start of the season!"

"Hi Sam. How are your grand-kids?" Miss May asked.

"Their pop makes the most delicious soft-serve in the universe. How do you think they are?"

Miss May laughed.

"Good point," I said. "Every kid dreams of having an ice cream legend for a grandpa."

Sam pointed at me. "I always knew you were the real genius of the sleuthing team. Miss May is only there for the looks."

Sam winked at Miss May. She blushed.

"Look! I made her blush. That's the highest compliment you could pay me. Just for that, ice cream's on the house."

Miss May giggled. I looked after her. That was one of the few times I'd ever seen Miss May flirt. Her blue eyes twinkled against her rouging cheeks. It was so cute, I started blushing too.

"What'll it be?" Sam asked.

Less than a minute later, I held in my hands the most beautiful ice cream cone I'd ever seen. Dipped in that chocolate sauce that hardens in about 30 seconds. Covered in crushed peanuts. Six inches high and swirled to perfection. Miss May got a medium cup with vanilla and chocolate swirl, hot fudge, whipped cream and a cherry. Then we promised Sam we'd be back soon and we strolled off toward town.

Admittedly, the first chunk of our conversation revolved around the incompatibility of Sandra Day O'Connor and Bruce Lee. The thought of those two cats together made both Miss May and I crack up. But the mayor's behavior at the press conference also concerned us. Liz's questions had flustered Mayor Delgado. And, as Miss May pointed out, the mayor had not denied any of Liz's accusations.

Was it possible that the scandal of Rosenberg's death ran all the way to the top of the Pine Grove government? The thought scared me. Even scarier? What if the scandal went higher than that? To the governor, or the president, or an unnamed foreign leader with plans to unravel American democracy, starting in suburban New York.

OK, my imagination needed a shorter leash. But the point is... We had more questions than answers. And that didn't feel good.

Miss May and I spent a few hours doing chores in town, so it was dark as we drove up Whitehill toward the orchard. It was a gorgeous night, but neither of us felt quite right. Questions filled our heads. Ice cream sloshed in our stomachs. And the steep climb toward the orchard did little to calm us.

I tried to measure my breathing and put my anxiety to rest with positive thinking, but no amount of positivity could have prepared me for what we discovered as we rumbled down the driveway toward the bake shop.

The front windows were shattered. The door was splintered and kicked in. A light flickered inside the shop.

Miss May's face turned white as she parked. "What in tarnation?"

She climbed out and rushed toward the shop. I followed, even queasier than I had been before.

As my feet crunched over the gravel I entertained the optimistic notion that perhaps there was an explanation for everything we had seen. But once inside the bakeshop, my worst fears were confirmed.

The alarm system flashed and whined. Donuts and baked goods were strewn everywhere. The cash register was split open and its contents were strewn across the floor.

I covered my mouth as I looked around, not sure if I was trying to suppress a scream or hold back vomit. And after a moment I mustered a few squeaky words. "Who would have done this?"

Miss May turned back to me. Face white. Hands trembling. When she spoke, her words were barely audible. "I have no idea."

I looked around and tried to stay calm. "Do you think this is connected to the murder? Is someone sending a signal?"

"There's one way we'll be able to tell for sure," Miss May said.

"What's that?" I asked.

Miss May crossed the bakeshop floor, stepped over some debris and entered the back office. I heard a rustling, and five seconds later her voice rang out from within. "I knew it!"

Miss May poked her head back out into the bakeshop. "They took the briefcase."

"Rosenberg's briefcase?"

"Of course, Chelsea. What other briefcase would I be talking about?"

"Sorry. Stupid question."

"No. I'm sorry," Miss May said. "I'm rattled. I shouldn't have snapped."

"But no one even knew we had the briefcase. Isn't it possible it's just a coincidence? Maybe the burglar took the briefcase just because it's a nice briefcase."

"There are no coincidences in investigations like these." Miss May picked up a lopsided chair and sat. Then she grabbed an apple cider donut off the floor and took a bite.

I laughed. "Good donut?"

Miss May nodded. "Big Dan's going to have to work hard if he wants to compete with me."

Miss May grabbed another chair off the floor and righted it. She patted the seat, and I crossed over and plopped down.

I grabbed my own donut off the floor and clinked it with Miss May's as if to say 'cheers.' Then I took a bite.

"I'm just saying," I said, with my mouth full. "There have been break-ins around town. Flanagan mentioned one at the meeting. And Petey's produce got stolen. So it's possible that this isn't connected to the murder."

"That's what they want you to think. Whoever did this staged it. Look around... My delicious donuts are tossed everywhere. The money from the cash register is gone. The burglar even took my antique signage off the walls. That stuff gets good money at antique shops."

"All of that seems like it was a genuine burglary. Not connected to the murder. That's what I'm saying."

"That's all just a cover so the cops don't make the connection."

"How do you know?"

"Because the door was kicked in."

"So what?"

"I forgot to lock it this morning," Miss May said. "No burglar would kick the door down instead of opening it right up. You would only do that if you were staging it to look like a break-in."

I sighed. "So you think this is the same person who killed Rosenberg? You think that's why someone went to the construction trailer that night? Looking for the briefcase?"

"That's an interesting theory," Miss May said. "Perhaps the killer never intended on murdering Rosenberg at all. They were just there for the briefcase. That would explain the struggle. The hasty escape."

"That's not my only theory," I said. "What if the mayor did this to send a signal? She didn't like our presence at that press conference."

"She didn't know we had the briefcase," Miss May said. "Otherwise, that's a sound theory too."

"Maybe she did know about the briefcase," I said. "Whoever did this has been following us. Or watching us somehow. Otherwise how would anyone have known we had the case?"

Miss May tilted her head, considering the sinister possibility that someone was stalking us. A stalker! "Well, whoever did steal it," I said, "joke's on them. KP used every trick in the proverbial book to open that case."

"Except opening it the right way," Miss May said. "Maybe whoever stole it has the proverbial key. Or the literal key."

I shuddered. The whole scenario chilled me, and I hated contemplating the evil genius behind the break-in.

Miss May got to her feet. "Toss that donut back onto the

floor and stand up. Whoever did this must have left a clue. It's up to us to find it."

"You really think we're going to find something in this mess?" I asked, finishing off the donut instead of throwing it back.

"Of course," Miss May said. "If we really look. Take this, for instance." Miss May squatted to get a close look at the floor. "Muddy footprints. Just like in Rosenberg's trailer."

I grabbed a cookie off the floor and held it up. "Here's a cookie with a bite taken out. But I don't see any teeth marks. Do you think that means our killer has no teeth?"

"Or they broke a piece off the cookie and ate it like that. Or the cookie broke when they tossed it."

"Good point," I said. "They should have offered a class in college about different ways criminals might eat a cookie. I mean, I know everything there is to know about the French Revolution and the warrior art of the Mesopotamian era, but I honestly thought for a few seconds that our killer might have no teeth."

Miss May laughed. "And that's what they call book smarts versus street smarts."

"Versus cookie smarts," I said.

"Lucky for you most people understand that there are different kinds of intelligence. I mean, take my doctor. She went to Oxford and last time I showed up for an appointment she had locked herself out of the office with the keys in her own pocket! Smart people do silly things. All the time."

We laughed. Then I heard a noise from the other room and froze. "Hey Miss May?"

Miss May looked over at me.

"... how do we know the burglar isn't still here?"

Miss May froze too. She gulped. "I guess we don't."

Miss May crossed behind the counter and pulled a butcher knife from a knife block. Her breathing got shallower. She handed me a rolling pin.

"Hello?" She looked under the counter. No one was there. "Anyone in here? Show yourself. We've got weapons."

Miss May flattened herself against the wall. I pancaked myself next to her, and we slinked toward the back office, one cautious, nerve-wracking step at a time.

Finally, we turned the corner. And my heart just about exploded out of my chest.

17

HUDSON HEART ATTACK

"*W*ayne! Thank goodness it's you." I rushed across the room and hugged Wayne so tight he gagged.

Miss May hung back by the door. She laughed. "All right, Chelsea. You're getting donut crumbs on Wayne's shirt."

I stepped back from the hug. *Yup*. Crumbs were every-where. "Oh no! I'm sorry."

"It's fine," Wayne said. "Just a little donut."

"It was a floor donut," I blurted. "I ate it off the floor."

Wayne laughed. "Not a big deal, Chels. Five second rule, right?"

"As far as I can tell it had been there all night. Thou-sands of seconds."

Miss May stepped forward. "OK, Chelsea. Everything's fine." She turned to Wayne. "We're shaken up from all this. Glad to see you. But surprised. I didn't even know you were back."

"Got back late last night. Your silent security alarm goes straight to the precinct. This is my first shift, and of course I wanted to answer this call." Wayne looked around the office and stepped out into the bakeshop. "So what happened in here?"

Miss May followed Wayne into the bakeshop. "What does it look like to you, Detective? It's a break-in."

Wayne surveyed the scene and shook his head.

Miss May continued. "The policing in this town has fallen apart since you left. Break-ins everywhere. And this is the most recent."

"What was that you said about the police work in this town?" Chief Flanagan entered through the main door of the bakeshop. She looked great, as always. Was her hair getting redder and softer with each passing day?

Miss May didn't back down. "You heard what I said, Chief. Unsolved break-ins. Murders that are not being investigated. Is that what you would call good police work?"

Flanagan crossed her arms. "Rosenberg's death was not a murder."

Right, and I didn't just eat a whole donut off the ground!

Miss May shook her head. "And I suppose you believe that this incident here has nothing to do with the fact that my niece and I have been uh, asking around about that 'not murder'?"

Sunshine nodded. "It's like you said. This is the most recent in a long string of break-ins. And as you can see, the Pine Grove Police Department is taking said break-ins seriously."

Flanagan crossed to Wayne and put her hand on his elbow. "Finish up in here and head outside, all right?"

Wayne shot a glance over to me. "Sure thing, Chief. Right behind you."

Flanagan looked around the bakeshop, shook her head, then strode outside.

"It's good to see you, Miss May," Wayne said. "Good to see you too, Chelsea. Although I wish it were under different circumstances."

"We all do, Detective." Miss May looked between me and Wayne. "I need to go to the ladies room. But you two should get reacquainted. Wayne, have you heard that Chelsea is being pursued by one of the new young bachelors in town?"

Wayne stammered. "Uh..."

Miss May smiled. "Good. You can talk about that."

Miss May smirked and exited. Her ability to be a romantic instigator, even in the most dire circumstances, impressed me. But I could have done without the casual reference to Germany Turtle. Even if I did infatuate the guy.

Once Miss May left, Wayne turned his full attention on me. I expected to fall into his blue-green eyes and tread water in the clear pool of his disarming gaze, as per usual. But he looked tired and haggard and I did not fall in.

"Your aunt cracks me up," Wayne said. "Isn't she scared with all this going on?"

I shrugged. "She doesn't get scared. Maybe she's a little rattled. But I'm the one who wears it on my sleeve."

"Please. You've come a long way," Wayne said. "Back when we met, you were such a crybaby."

"Hey! I was a new girl in a new place. Facing my first murder ever!"

Wayne laughed. "I'm just saying. I don't think you're such a scaredy-cat anymore. I mean, we're standing in an active crime scene right now and as far as I know you haven't cried once."

I smiled. "Nope. I shoved my tears down with donuts and courage."

Wayne smirked but it faded. "This is kind of alarming, though. No pun intended. You're sure you're okay?"

"I'm good. I promise."

Wayne nodded. Looked around. "I called you."

I looked down. "I called you back."

"This trial, being a witness, the whole thing... It's been draining."

I kicked at some debris on the floor. "I get it."

"We should do something though," Wayne said. "You feel like dancing?"

I flicked my eyes up at him. "You're back in town for good now?"

Wayne nodded. "Thankfully. Yes. I mean, as far as I know."

"Good."

"Good indeed." Wayne joined me in the awkward sport of kicking at the ground. "Hey, uh... What are you and Miss May thinking about this Rosenberg thing? And all these break-ins?"

I raised my eyebrows. "Is the great Detective Wayne Hudson asking me for inside information on a police investigation?"

Wayne shrugged. "It's not a police investigation if the police are not investigating. All I'm doing is asking you for a little Pine Grove gossip."

I smiled. "However you want to justify it to yourself, Detective."

Wayne sighed. "Do you know anything or not, Chelsea?"

I glanced toward the entrance to the bakeshop to make sure Flanagan wasn't too close. "OK. Here's the gossip. Word is, this was no accident. The mayor might be corrupt. The police chief might be corrupt. And the most hated man in town is dead but no clear suspect has emerged. A pair of talented and beautiful amateur sleuths are on the case, but they've got no safety net now that their reliable sidekick in the police force is tethered to an unreasonable chief and seems to have lost the ability to think for himself."

"Hilarious," Wayne said. "But I'm no sidekick. And I can still think for myself. Why do you think I'm asking about all this?"

"Whatever you say."

Flanagan kicked the broken door open And stood in the frame like a warrior princess. "Wayne. Outside?"

Flanagan exited and Wayne followed. He turned back before he left. "By the way... Who's this new eligible bachelor Miss May was talking about?"

I blushed and looked down. "No one."

"Your cheeks get that red over no one?"

I looked up with a straight face. "It's no one. Trust me."

That night, I crawled into bed and fell fast asleep. But I woke up a few hours later to the sound of a tapping on my window. I rolled over, trying to ignore the noise. But it persisted.

Tap tap. Tap tap.

I checked my clock. 2 AM. What the heck?

Tap tap. Tap tap.

I turned on my bedside lamp and crossed to the window. I saw nothing outside. But then I heard the noise again.

Tap tap. Tap tap.

I grabbed the window and slid it open with a quiet fwshhhhh.

The only sound for miles was the wind rustling through the apple trees. No one was out there. So what was that incessant tapping?

I was about to close the window when I noticed a small

figurine, about two inches high, perched on the sill of the window.

It was a small, gold-trimmed calico cat figurine, with a little red fist knocking in a perpetual motion.

I recognized the figurine from my art history courses as a "maneki neko," a common Japanese figurine meant to bring good luck.

Over the years I had noticed similar talismans at the entrance to almost every sushi restaurant I had ever patronized, the little cats' knocking fists beckoning customers to enter.

But I had never held one of the little calico figurines in my hands until that night.

As I lifted the kitty from the windowsill, its weight surprised me. The figurine was not plastic, like most maneki neko cats that I had seen. Instead, the little kitty in my hands was metal. Maybe even gold-plated.

I held the cat up to my eyes to get a better look. And I couldn't help but speak to it in my "talking to cute animals voice."

"Well hello there," I said, scrunching up my nose. "Aren't you a cute little one? How did you end up on my windowsill? Did you get cold out there? You're an itty-bitty little kitty aren't you?"

"Who the heck are you talking to?"

I shrieked and fell back on my behind. I looked up at Miss May towering above me.

I smiled. "I found a cat."

"Oh. Is it a he? Potential partner for Sandra Day O'Connor?"

I held up the little metal kitty, "I'm not sure he's her type."

Miss May and I decided the maneki neko could be a

clue. So we spent the next few minutes trying to solve the mini mystery of the mini cat. But the darn thing was inscrutable.

We asked questions. We poked at the kitty. We picked it up and shook it. In some contexts, I'm sure the zen, meditative spirit of the animal was relaxing and calming. But in the heat of a murder investigation, we felt as though we were being taunted by the persistent pawing of the metallic minx.

After fifteen minutes, Miss May and I were still convinced the cat was a clue. But neither of us could figure out who would have left it. Nor could we discern what the clue was.

We were about to give up when I noticed a very tiny latch on the back of the cat. I got tweezers and pried the latch open. Inside was a small battery compartment with a watch battery. The little circular ones that are so hard to find when you need them.

When I removed the watch battery, I saw a minuscule white sticker with microscopic writing printed on the surface.

"What does it say?" Miss May asked.

I leaned in to get a closer look. But there was no way I could read the writing. "I don't know. I can't read that! The font is like Times New Roman negative twelve."

"You know what this means?" Miss May smiled.

I shrugged. "That my bright, young eyes are not as strong as you expected them to be?"

Miss May exited and returned a few seconds later, carrying a small wooden box.

"This means that tonight is the first night in our careers of amateur sleuths that we have an occasion to use...a magnifying glass!"

Miss May beamed.

I laughed. "That's what you're so excited about? A magnifying glass?"

"Of course! This is a rite of passage. Every sleuth has their first magnifying glass case. We've arrived, baby! Now scoot over and let me try this thing on for size."

Miss May leaned over the maneki neko and used the magnifying glass to get a better look at the inscription on the tiny sticker.

I edged up next to her. "Well? What does it say?"

Miss May lowered the magnifying glass and looked at me. "It's an address." She took a deep breath and let it out. "In New York City."

18

RENT DESTABILIZED

*T*he next morning, Teeny drove us down to Manhattan in her stylish death machine. *Oops, did I say death machine?* I meant convertible.

I would go into great detail about how Teeny captained her convertible like a madwoman. Slowing to a crawl in the fast lane because she thought she saw a deer. Yelling at a driver who she was convinced "gave her a look." Going in reverse on the highway after she missed her exit. But the drive was so beautiful, I did my best to ignore the multiple near-death experiences and focus on the scenery instead.

We started off on the Taconic Parkway, surrounded on every side by tall, green trees. In a few months, those stately oaks and maples would change to fiery reds and oranges, but at that point, they were a deep emerald. Then we jumped on the Westside Drive. The Hudson River rolled by on our right. The beginnings of New York City sprouted up on our left. And Teeny played her "New York City Mix" on the stereo.

The playlist kicked off with "New York, New York" by Frank Sinatra. Then "New York State of Mind," by Billy Joel. After that came a few rap songs, all with New York in the title. It surprised me to hear hip-hop on Teeny's mix, but she waved my doubts away. "I'm hip to the new sounds," she insisted. "I don't like 'em, but I know 'em."

As we drove, I tried to mentally prepare for what we might find at the mystery address. Last time we'd followed a clue into the city, it had been a valuable lead but a bizarre experience. And I wondered what this venture would hold.

I looked down at my hand, where I'd written the address in permanent marker just in case we all forgot it.

15 Waverly Pl., #1B
    New York, NY 10003

Teeny saw me checking the address. "Do you think it's an apartment or a business?"

"I think it's an apartment, based on what I saw online," I said. "But there wasn't much information available."

· · ·

"Whatever it is," Miss May said. "We need to keep our composure."

I leaned forward from the back seat. "Do you think this place could be dangerous?"

Miss May craned her neck to meet my eyes. "It's possible. Someone is dead, after all."

"We'll be fine," Teeny said. "I brought protection just in case."

Miss May and I exchanged a nervous look.

"What do you mean by that?" I asked.

Teeny dug in her purse without taking her eyes off the wheel. She pulled out lipstick, a pair of sandals, a pair of tennis shoes, and a jar labeled "emergency sprinkles," but nothing that seemed like it could protect us if the situation turned frightening.

"What are you looking for in there?" I asked.

"One second!" Teeny kept digging. "I wanted to bring

pepper spray but I didn't have any. So I grabbed this instead."

Miss May and I exchanged another concerned glance. Then Teeny pulled a large spray can from her purse and thrust it into the air with a triumphant fist pump.

"Found it!"

Teeny handed the spray to Miss May.

"Teeny. This is olive oil cooking spray."

Teeny smiled. "You think you spray that in someone's eyes, it's not going to slow them down?"

"I guess it would," Miss May said. "But not for long."

"Plus we can spray it on stairs if we want to make the bad guys slip and fall," Teeny said.

"The can's not even full," I said. "I don't think we can coat a flight of stairs with it!"

. . .

"Yeah," Miss May agreed. "I say our best strategy in the face of danger is to flee."

"You can run," Teeny said. "While I stay back and fight."

Miss May handed the spray back to Teeny. "We're just heading down for some research. I'm sure we'll be fine. Remember the last time we came to the city? We thought we were about to come face to face with an attacker, and it was a squirrel!"

I chuckled. "The squirrel attacked Teeny!"

"And if that bushy-tailed terror comes back for more, this time I've got my spray!" Once again, Teeny hoisted her olive oil spray in the air.

"I don't think olive oil is a squirrel repellent," Miss May laughed. "But I hope this place is nothing like that sketchy apartment. I hated it there."

I looked out the window to my left. The skyscrapers of midtown Manhattan loomed above us. The intimidating buildings sent a shiver down my spine.

. . .

I hope everything goes OK today, I thought. *Because I don't have a license to use cooking spray as a weapon.*

By 10 AM, we were in the heart of Greenwich Village, one of New York's most exclusive neighborhoods, surrounded by quaint brick buildings and cobblestone streets.

According to the map on my phone, we were only a few minutes from our destination. So we parked the car in the first available spot, and followed the little voice directing us from my phone.

First, we took a short cut through one of my favorite spots in Manhattan, Washington Square Park. The park was even more wondrous than I remembered.

Jazz musicians played quiet love songs under hundred-year-old trees. College girls sunbathed on the far lawn. A portly man sold hot dogs from a cart. NYU students read beside the central fountain, quintessential young learners in action.

When we emerged on the other side of the park, we found ourselves on a quaint tree-lined street with small, charming brick buildings.

Even though I was happy I didn't live or work in Manhattan anymore, I had never fallen out of love with the Big Apple.

The atmosphere that day had me swooning with love for New York City all over again.

The sound of the GPS lady cut my nostalgia short with a loud bing. "You have arrived at your destination."

When I looked up, I saw she was right. We were standing at the foot of 15 Waverly Place. What I saw surprised me.

Unlike much of the surrounding area, 15 Waverly was a modern structure. A dozen stories of steel and glass, with reflective windows and a shiny exterior.

During my time as an interior designer, I had trained myself to find value in almost any aesthetic. And I had learned to love many peculiar buildings and homes. But I could find few redeeming qualities in 15 Waverly Place.

Large, imposing and ugly, it had none of the soul or charm of the smaller brick buildings in the village. Instead it evoked a cold and cruel invader, descended from outer space to devour all semblance of attractive architecture.

I don't use this word lightly, but the building was a monstrosity.

. . .

"Holy momma," Teeny said. "This building is hideous. Are we sure this is the right place?"

I nodded. "This is it. What should we do now?"

Miss May pointed out a sign posted on the door of the building.

TOUR YOUR FUTURE HOME TODAY.
    COME INSIDE.

"It's an apartment complex," she said. "Something tells me we won't run into any squirrels in there."

A perky salesgirl approached as soon as we entered the building. She was wearing a tight black dress with high heels. She had perfect makeup, complete with cherry red lipstick. And her bright white teeth glimmered in the light.

The girl clutched her heart like she pitied us as she spoke. "Oh I'm sorry ladies, are you lost? The soup kitchen is 15 East Waverly, not West Waverly."

Teeny and Miss May scoffed in unison. I couldn't tell who was more offended. But I spotted Teeny reaching into her purse for the olive oil.

· · ·

Miss May narrowed her eyes. "Come again?"

The salesgirl spoke louder, like she thought maybe Miss May didn't speak good English.

"Soup kitchen. East Waverly. Not here. Bye now!"

The girl click-clacked across the lobby and held the door open for us to leave. Neither Miss May nor Teeny budged. I smirked, excited to see what might happen next.

"We're not here for soup," Miss May said. "We're here to find out about our future home. Like the sign on the door suggests?"

The salesgirl stammered. Teeny took a step toward her. "That's right. We read the sign on the door all by ourselves. We can do our timetables too. And the young one can recite the state capitals by heart."

"That's right," I said. "Did you know Augusta is the capital of Maine? Most people think it's Portland."

The salesgirl blinked a few times, shocked. "That's... great. So you ladies are here for a tour of the complex?"

. . .

Miss May nodded. "Yup."

Throughout the tour, Teeny, Miss May, and I refused to acknowledge the grandeur of the building's interior.

None of us wanted to give the annoying salesgirl the satisfaction.

But the space was magnificent.

The basement had an Olympic-sized swimming pool, a sauna, a steam room, and a hot tub.

The roof deck had gorgeous outdoor furniture. Chaise lounges with durable, luxurious pillows. Long, elegant fire pits for the winter. And barbecues that the salesgirl was careful to point out had come from the direct recommendation of an award-winning celebrity chef who "could not be named."

The model apartment had sixteen-foot ceilings, elegant mid-century modern furniture, and a TV in the bathroom.

And every resident we saw was just as beautiful as the building itself.

·   ·   ·

In the gym, attractive people lifted weights without breaking a sweat. In the business center, attractive people typed on fancy laptops. In the lounge, attractive people sipped on fresh-brewed lattes and made nonchalant conversation.

The whole building had a bit of a Stepford vibe. But not in a murderous way. More like in the "rich people are taking over the world and making everything the same" way.

Toward the end of the tour, Miss May asked if we could see apartment 1B, and the salesgirl looked confused.

"We don't have an apartment 1B. That would be a basement apartment. And as I've shown you, our basement contains a gym and a lounge. Not an apartment."

Miss May narrowed her eyes. "Are you sure there's not—"

"Never." The salesgirl hardened. "We would never put an apartment in the basement of this building."

"OK," Miss May said. "Sorry for asking."

The salesgirl smiled. "Not a problem. Now if you'll excuse me, I have another tour set to begin shortly. Such a pleasure meeting you."

. . .

The woman hurried back toward her office, but Miss May called out before the salesgirl got across the room.

"One last question?"

The woman turned back. "How can I help?"

"When was this place built?"

The woman rolled her eyes. "We've been open sixteen months. Can't you smell the new?"

"I guess I can smell it," Miss May said. "And do you know what stood on this lot before they built this place?

The woman crinkled her nose. "Rent-stabilized housing. Section 8. This is so much nicer, don't you think?"

"This certainly is luxurious," Miss May said.

"Hold on." I stepped forward. "Isn't rent-stabilized housing for people that don't have a lot of money? Where did they all go?"

. . .

The salesgirl shrugged. "I don't know. New Jersey?"

The girl's phone rang. "I have to take this. No more questions. Bye!"

We watched the salesgirl slip into her office and close the door. Then Miss May turned to me. "I know where at least one person who used to live here went."

"Where?" I asked.

Miss May looked me square in the eye. "Pine Grove."

19

WATCHING WALLACE

*T*hat night, we went looking for Wallace in town. We found him in the middle of what appeared to be a one-person ballroom dance on the sidewalk outside the *Brown Cow*.

Sure, Wallace looked ridiculous dancing. But the guy had undeniably great dance moves.

He could do the robot. And the moonwalk. And he could pop and lock like J Lo at a sold-out show. If he didn't also have a penchant for angry outbursts, I would have joined him that day for a Viennese Waltz. But I was afraid of Wallace. So I stayed in the VW Bus with Miss May and enjoyed his dancing from afar.

"I can't believe Wallace used to live in apartment 1B," Teeny said. "Are you two a million percent positive about that?"

Miss May nodded. "Chelsea confirmed it online last night."

"And Rosenberg led the team that tore down the Section 8 housing where Wallace lived? You confirmed that too?" Teeny asked.

I nodded. "Yup."

"So what now?" Teeny asked. "We found the guy. Are we going to sit here all day or are we going to question him?"

"This is a stakeout," Miss May said. "We're going to watch. Learn. See if we can gather more information that confirms our theory."

"And the theory is that Wacky Wallace killed Rosenberg because Rosenberg destroyed Wallace's home in the city?" Teeny asked.

Miss May shrugged. "Kind of. Yeah. But Wallace is not the type of guy you approach on the street and interrogate out of nowhere."

Teeny sighed. "Poor guy. With moves like that, he should have been a reality TV dance star. Not a small-town killer."

"If only he'd been born a generation later maybe he would be on TV," I said. "He has terrific moves."

Across the street, Wallace had morphed his ballroom dance into an impromptu 60's routine. He did the Egyptian, he held his nose and wiggled underwater, and he bopped his head in time with imaginary music.

"How did you find where someone lives on your phone, anyway?" Teeny asked. "I thought that stuff was private."

"I found a post Wallace made in an online forum. He used to hold meetings in apartment 1B for his 'Military Fantasy Book Club' and he had been looking for new members."

"'Military Fantasy?' That's a whole genre of books?" Teeny said. "Who has fantasies about the military? I have fantasies about fuzzy blankets and winning the lottery."

Miss May chuckled. "To each her own."

Teeny shook out her arms like she had gotten a chill. "Gives me a bad feeling. That guy being into military stuff."

"Maybe he likes the historical aspect," I said.

"Yeah right," Teeny said.

Out the window, Wallace stopped dancing and screamed at the passing cars. He didn't say much, but his face was red and he clenched his fists.

Just at that moment, Germany Turtle approached Wallace's position from a few feet away, licking an ice cream cone and listening to music on his headphones. Germany stopped when he spotted Wallace, but it was too late. Wallace spun on the poor, defenseless Turtle with crazed, angry eyes. We couldn't hear what Wallace said, but we watched the entire scene play out from our spot in the VW bus.

Wallace took a few steps toward Germany. Germany stumbled backward and raised his hands in surrender. Wallace kept advancing, and Germany tripped over his own feet. We cringed as Germany lost his grip on the ice cream cone, and a perfectly good scoop of strawberry plopped to the ground.

"What a waste of ice cream," Teeny said.

"Poor kid," Miss May said. "Look at him. Terrified. You'd think being around all those lions would have toughened him up."

"Maybe he's right to be terrified," I said. "If Wallace is a killer, shouldn't we try to help or call someone or something?"

Miss May shook her head. "Nah. The Turtle is getting back in his shell. See?"

We watched as Germany hurried over to a parked car, one of those tiny clown cars like they have in Europe. Germany got in and drove away.

Teeny laughed. "Turtle back in his shell! Look at that funny little car!"

"Germany is so silly," I said, shaking my head. "Not mean like his parents, but just as weird."

Miss May turned to Teeny. "Don't you think he'd be good for Chelsea?"

Teeny shook her head. "No way. I'm Team Wayne. I like my men tall and tough."

"And bearded?" I asked with a sly grin.

"Beards are fine, if they're done right," Teeny said. *I don't think she got the reference to Big Dan.*

Wallace shook his fist in anger and yelled as Germany pulled away and disappeared down Main Street.

"What do you think Wallace is saying?" I asked.

"Let's find out." Miss May rolled the window down and we could hear Wallace with perfect clarity.

"Stupid idiot kid! Don't just leave the ice cream on the ground. It's still good. A little dirt, sure. But it's healthy to eat dirt! Builds up the immune system."

Teeny tsk-tsked. "Healthy dirt? This guy is nuts."

"That's true," I said. "Especially for babies. The more dirt babies eat, the stronger their immune systems are later in life."

Teeny rolled her eyes. "Save it for *Jeopardy*, Chelsea."

I shrugged. "Fine. I will. But you better be nice or I won't share my winnings with you. Or take you on my victory cruise."

Teeny looked over at me, "Awwww, I want to go on the cruise."

I laughed. "OK. You can come."

Over the next hour, we stayed parked, watching Wallace. At one point, he almost got hit by a car. Then he almost got hit by a bus. He also chased Sudeer across the road, screaming about the atrocities that Massive Mart would bring upon the town.

Finally, Chief Flanagan showed up and scared Wallace off the corner. Miss May put the VW bus in gear and slowly followed Wallace as he trudged toward the outskirts of town.

"What are we doing now?" Teeny asked.

"Stakeout, part two. Following the suspect to see what he reveals."

"We're in a giant yellow bus," Teeny said. "You don't think he notices us?"

Wallace did a spin move, then grabbed his crotch like Michael Jackson.

"Anyone else? I'd say you have a good point," Miss May said. "But Wallace is too distracted for that."

"Do you think Wallace is also the thief who's been hitting businesses around town?" I asked.

Miss May shrugged. "I'm not sure. It seems like he had a decent motive for killing Rosenberg. But I don't quite see a motive for the burglaries."

"I see a motive," Teeny said. "The guy doesn't seem like he has much money. Maybe he steals stuff and then sells it on the black market."

"I don't know if there's a black market for Petey's farm to table produce," I said.

"I bet he ate that stuff," Teeny said.

Miss May pointed out the window. "Look. He's walking up into the woods."

Sure enough, Wallace was trudging up a steep hill into a thick patch of trees outside town. Teeny opened her door and slipped one foot out of the van. "So let's go. Let's follow him up there!"

Miss May shook her head. "I'm not sure I want to follow a suspected killer into the forest."

"Why not?" Teeny said. "I've got my olive oil spray."

Miss May kept her eyes trained on Wallace as he marched further into the forest. "It's almost dark. We'll head up there first chance we get. When it's daylight."

"And maybe when we know Wallace is in town," I suggested. "So we won't get ambushed once we get up there."

"Exactly." Miss May lingered a few more seconds as Wallace disappeared into the forest. Then she put the bus back in gear, and we headed home.

20

OUT OF THE SHELL

*T*hat night, Miss May and I baked a few batches of her famous apple pie cookies, aka Appie Oaters, to sell that weekend in the shop.

It pleased me when Miss May put me in charge of the apples instead of the dough. Over the years, I had done both jobs, but the apples were always more fun to prepare than the dough.

I began by selecting the perfect combination of sweet and tangy apples. After I peeled and chopped, I caramelized the whole batch in coconut oil, brown sugar, cinnamon, and nutmeg using one of Miss May's enormous frying pans.

Before long, the entire bake shop filled with the smell of apples and spices, all forming into a delicious syrup in the pan.

I tasted the mix and closed my eyes to savor the flavor. The apples were soft. And the brown sugar sauce was just sweet enough to emphasize the tartness in the apples without overwhelming it.

I took another taste. And then another. *OK. I had a bunch*

of tastes. Then I combined the apples with Miss May's dough and we balled the cookies and set them to bake.

As we worked, I tried several times to bring up the investigation, but Miss May wasn't feeling very talkative.

"I don't have the answers, Chelsea," she said. "We need to find out what Wallace is doing up in the forest. Once we get that information, we'll know what to do."

"But—"

"But there's nothing else to talk about," Miss May said. "Why don't you relax? Take a bath."

"Why?" I asked. "Am I sweaty? Do I smell? I took a shower this morning."

Miss May laughed. "You don't smell. I just meant... It might be useful to take our minds off the investigation for a bit. Often when you relax your brain, good ideas show up unprompted."

"I can't relax my brain on command. My brain does what it wants. It has a mind of its own!"

Miss May set a timer for the cookies. "Fine. I'll take a bath."

Once the cookies had finished baking, I walked out to the barn to visit my friend, See-Saw the tiny horse.

On prior investigations, I'd had important breakthroughs while chatting with See-Saw. I was hoping for a similar talk that night, but like my aunt, See-Saw wasn't in the mood to discuss the investigation. The more I discussed the details of the case, the louder she chewed.

But then I brought up my encounter with the illustrious Detective Wayne Hudson and her ears perked up. See-Saw listened as I told her how I had run into Wayne at the bakeshop. But when I mentioned that he asked me on a date, she gave a disapproving snort.

"What's with the snort," I said. "You don't like Wayne anymore?"

See-Saw stamped her hooves.

"I know he's been unavailable," I said. "But it was a work thing! And we had that amazing dance. Remember? We have such good chemistry. Shouldn't I see where the relationship goes?"

Another stamp from See-Saw. She was not feeling Wayne that evening.

"That's true," I agreed. "He has shut me out of every case. But he's a cop, what would it look like if he invited civilians to take part in his investigations?"

Stamp. Snort.

"I know. You're right. He doesn't give me or Miss May credit, even when we're the ones who solve the mysteries. But I kind of like Wayne's stubborn side. He's a proud guy. People say that was how my dad was."

See-Saw turned back to her oats. She wasn't in the mood to talk dead parents that night, and I couldn't blame her.

"Maybe I should give Wayne a call," I said. "What you think about that?"

See-Saw didn't look up. I pulled out my phone and scrolled to Wayne's name. And I was about to hit call when I heard footsteps behind me.

I turned just as Germany Turtle entered the barn holding a bouquet of roses. "My goodness. You're more beautiful in the moonlight than in the light of the karate dojo."

I blushed. I couldn't help it. Ugh. Germany's lines were cringe-y but so sincere.

"Germany. Hi."

"May I come in?"

I gestured to See-Saw. "That's up to her. I'm just a visitor here."

Germany entered with a smile. "My! What a wonderful animal. Is this a baby horse or a child horse?"

I laughed. "This is our tiny horse, See-Saw. Have you never seen a tiny horse before?"

"I'm sad to say I have not. The wildlife of Africa is diverse but usually quite large. Not tiny at all. A horse like this would be eaten by the lions instantly. Reduced to a cavity of bones to be picked at by the buzzards and hyenas on the Sahara."

See-Saw looked up and whinnied. She didn't like Germany's candor.

"I'm being rude, aren't I?" Germany said. "I'm sorry, See-Saw. I would never want the pride to eat you."

Germany reached out a tentative hand to pet See-Saw. She nudged her nose into Germany's palm. He gave a delighted gasp.

"My! What a nice equine. I heard you chatting with her earlier. I hope it's all right that I interrupted. I knocked upon the door of your farmhouse and had a wonderful interaction with your aunt. She offered me a fresh baked cookie, the likes of which even the most accomplished bakers in Paris and Milan shall never match."

"That's a very flattering way to talk about Miss May's Appie Oaters," I said. "I helped her make them."

"Don't tell me that," said Germany. "My admiration for you is already overwhelming."

I looked at Germany. "Are you for real?"

"What do you mean? Is that a question of my existential identity? Because I have given the matter a lot of thought and I have decided that, like the Velveteen Rabbit, I will only become real when all my buttons and whiskers have been loved off. Preferably by you."

Germany smiled, and I burst into giggles. I couldn't help it. Germany was too much. *Just too much!* I cleared my throat and awkwardly shifted the conversation away from the young Turtle's affections.

"So you had a nice chat with Miss May, huh?"

"Oh yes. She is kind but intimidating. Is it true she was the most formidable prosecutor at all of New York City?"

"That's what I've heard." I'd also heard otherwise, but I would not get into that. "But I've only ever known her as a baker. And kind of a mom."

"Ah yes. Fellow orphans." Germany held up his palm, and I realized he was going for a high-five.

"You want to high-five over being orphans?"

"I have heard high-fives are used as an expression of solidarity or camaraderie. Inappropriate in this instance?"

I laughed. "Kind of, yeah."

Germany lowered his hand. "Ah. Well. Now I feel a fool. Perhaps I should leave you here to continue your deeply personal conversation with See-Saw the tiny horse."

I turned redder than a ripe Red Delicious. "You heard that?"

"Only the last part, about whether you should contact the large detective via telephone. My vote would be no, as you might imagine." Germany noticed my flushing cheeks. "It's nothing to be embarrassed about. I wish I had a horse in which I could confide. Tiny or regular-sized."

I picked up a handful oats and fed them to See-Saw. Germany resumed petting her.

"You could confide in See-Saw," I said. "If you want to. I don't want to hog her wisdom."

"Oh. Then perhaps I will." Germany grabbed a handful

oats and stepped closer to See-Saw. "Hello horse. Please accept this as my formal invitation to enter a friendship. I'm new in town, and recently de-parented. So I am seeking meaningful connections to salve my wounds."

Woof! That got personal real fast.

When I had first arrived in Pine Grove, I'd had a bad habit of crying constantly. I had gotten over that habit, but at that moment, I had to fight to swallow the lump in my throat. Germany Turtle was getting my emotional goat. *Or my emotional tiny horse, I guess.*

"You're lucky to have such a wonderful companion in See-Saw," Germany said.

He and I made eye contact.

"Chelsea, there's something you should know," Germany said. "And it's that I find you fascinating. Funny and smart. Perhaps not street smart but book smart. I like that. The streets confound me as well. I also find you charming and beautiful. And I think your love for this tiny horse speaks volumes about the merit of your character. Frankly, I would like to date you. You may have understood that already, based on our first interaction. But I wanted to state it clearly now."

I wasn't sure what to say or do in response to Germany's declaration. Yes, he'd already made it clear that he liked me. But something about that moment, standing there with him, in the barn, listening to his unabashed praise, gave me butterflies. *Or were they moths?* I stammered, unable to find the right words.

"You don't need to say anything," Germany continued. "Not yet. I'm not proposing marriage. I'm not professing wild, moonstruck love, however much I might want to. I'm a romantic at heart. But I am telling you that I'm working on my muscle tone. Soon I too will be a hunk of sizzling beef with a side of more beef and beef for dessert. Just like your detective. And I'm opening a tutor shop in town. So I will be fully employed in short order. The tutor shop will be called Germany's German Tutor Shop and it will be a great success."

My inner know-it-all kicked in, and I found my voice. "Do you mean like a tutoring service? Like where you're a teacher? I don't think they call those shops."

"Oh. Yes. That's what I mean."

I laughed. "How did you decide on German? Pine Grove High doesn't even offer classes in German."

"Interesting," Germany said. "I don't speak German, either. I liked the name. Perhaps I should open another business?"

"Don't ask me! My business was a disaster." Well, it had been a success until my runaway fiancé had stolen it. But still...

"Perhaps I could volunteer," Germany said. "My parents, although they struggled with money toward the end, squir-reled away significant funds for my inheritance and had a substantial life insurance policy. So I'm not in dire need of opening a tutor shop or any other shop."

See-Saw stamped and turned in a circle.

"That appears to be my cue," Germany said. "The tiny horse has tired of my pontificating. Alas, I shall alight back to my home on foot. May I hug you as a platonic friend?"

"No one has ever asked me that before," I said.

"Well," Germany said. "You don't have to answer now. Think about it. For next time. And whatever you do in this investigation of the Rosenberg slaying... Please maintain your safety as a top priority."

I nodded. "I'll do my best."

21

HOT SAUCE AND HAVOC

*T*he next morning, our mission was to trek up into the forest to figure out what Wallace had been doing up there. But first we had to make sure he was somewhere in town, that way we'd know the coast was clear in the forest.

Our first stop? Miss May and I met Teeny for breakfast at *Peter's Land and Sea*. But before we entered the restaurant, Petey exploded out the front door with a scream.

"I can't do this! I quit. I want to go back to high school!"

Petey froze when he saw us, then jumped back into his 'restauranteur' persona. "Oh. Greetings, ladies. Here to join us for breakfast? Right this way."

"Not so fast, Petey," Teeny said. "You can't pretend we didn't see that."

"Oh. That? I was just blowing off steam. Not a big deal."

Teeny put her hand on Petey's arm. "Petey. It's OK. You can talk to us."

Petey's lip quivered. "Fine. I'm overwhelmed! I can't do this. I'm not a restauranteur. I didn't even graduate from high school."

Teeny shook her head. "You are a restauranteur, Petey. Look at this place. It's beautiful. And you were the best employee I ever had. Also, you're a better cook than me! I'm a genius with recipes, but your execution is superb."

Petey kicked the ground. "That's a lie. You're the best cook in Pine Grove."

"But I can't do fancy stuff like you," Teeny said. "Listen, I get it. Running a restaurant can be overwhelming. But you're doing solid work. You just need to stay calm and take it one dish at a time."

"You think so?" Petey asked.

Teeny nodded. "The first few weeks after I took over *Grandma's* from my mom, I was an absolute mess. I didn't get any orders right. I bought two hundred gallons of expired milk. My hair-clip fell out and I baked it into someone's quiche. But then things got easier. And it all turned around. The same thing will happen to you."

Petey stood a little taller. "Maybe you're right. Maybe I can do this. You think I can do this?"

"We all do, son," Miss May said. "But right now you need to turn around. Your kitchen is smoking."

Petey turned around. Sure enough, smoke plumed from the kitchen. Petey bolted inside like a roadrunner.

"You really think he'll be okay?" I asked.

"I do," Teeny said. "But I'm not going to eat in there today. What do you say? *Brown Cow* for a cup of coffee and a chocolate chip muffin?"

Miss May and I nodded, and we turned and walked in the other direction as the fire alarm blared from inside *Peter's Land and Sea.*

I smiled as we entered the shop. My favorite barista, Rita, was working behind the counter. Her co-worker, Willow, cleaned tables in the seating area.

A few of our prior investigations had involved Rita, and she was always good for the most recent Pine Grove gossip. Plus, she usually had adorable photos of her little baby, Vinny Jr., on her phone. And she made my coffee drinks just right. Light on the coffee, heavy on the cream. And sugar. And whipped cream. And did I mention sugar?

I asked Rita if she had seen Wallace the Traveler in town that morning and she shrugged. "Most days that guy is out on the street before we open. But not today. You ask me it's a refreshing change of pace. The guy can dance but he's vulgar."

Willow called out from across the room. "I haven't seen him either!"

A few minutes later, I reconvened with Teeny and Miss May. Each had spoken to other townspeople but neither had information about Wallace's whereabouts.

"If he's not in town, he must still be up in the forest," Miss May said.

"So let's go get him!" Teeny clenched her little fist with determination.

"I don't want to go up there if he's lurking in the trees." I lowered my voice. "Wallace might be the killer. It's not safe."

"Oh yes it is." Teeny pulled a large bottle of hot sauce from her purse. "This stuff is way more potent than the olive oil spray. One splash in the eyes? Blinded for life."

I opened my mouth to list all the reasons hot sauce was an inadequate means of self-defense, but Miss May spoke before I had the chance. "We waited this long. We might as well hang out a few more hours. Once Wallace shows up in town, we'll follow his path up into the woods. And we won't need to blind anyone with any condiments."

"Fine," Teeny said. "But I'm ordering scrambled eggs. I'm going to use this hot sauce for something."

By the time Teeny finished her eggs, there was still no sign of Wallace, and everyone in town seemed to have noticed his disappearance.

Arthur, the owner of the gas station, commented that he hoped Wallace had moved somewhere new. Petunia agreed. A few others remarked that they missed Wallace's dance moves but not his angry outbursts. And the consensus was that Wallace's absence was a good thing.

But the longer Wallace stayed missing, the more anxious Miss May, Teeny, and I became. Only we knew that Wallace was the number one suspect in Rosenberg's murder. So only we knew that Wallace's absence could portend something devious.

We feared that Wallace might have detected our stakeout the prior night. Maybe he'd made a run for it. Worse yet, maybe he was disposing of evidence. Worse even still, what if Wallace had moved on to his next victim?

After a few hours of patience, all three of us had grown weary of waiting.

"We can't sit around until Wallace makes a run for it," I said. "We should go see what's up in that forest. Or tell the police what we know."

Miss May shook her head. "Chief Flanagan has no interest in solving this murder. Whatever happens next, it's up to us."

"So do you think we should go up there?" I asked.

"We should have gone up five hours ago," Teeny said. "I wasted half my weaponized hot sauce on my eggs. If we wait much longer I won't have any left for blinding."

Miss May nodded. "Okay. Let's head up now, while we still have plenty of light left in the day. If we spot him, we'll act like we're up there on an innocent hike."

"And what's our plan if he tries to kill us?" I asked.

Miss May shrugged. "We run."

Teeny hoisted the hot sauce in the air. "Or we fight."

Neither option made me feel great. But the plan was in motion. So I leaned in.

The path that Wallace took up the hill started on the side of the road and cut into the trees after a few feet. Wallace's footsteps had flattened the grass near the road. But once the path took us past the first thicket of bushes, the forest grew dense on all sides. And the streets and stores of Pine Grove felt hours away after less than a minute of walking.

"The forest is so green," I said. "You never see this color in the city. I missed it."

Teeny swatted at her arm. "Did you miss the mosquitoes too?"

"We had mosquitoes. Just not the forests," I said.

"Gross," Teeny said. "That's like having coffee with no sugar."

"Or cream." Miss May reached into her purse and pulled out a bottle of bug spray. "Here. Don't use it all. We may need it for blinding our foes."

Teeny took the spray with a sardonic "har-har" and applied the repellent in a broad sweeping motion over her body. She handed me the bottle, and I went through the same ritual.

We walked a few more steps, then I spotted a few does and fawns up the path about twenty feet. The does were alert, ears twitching and eyes wide. The fawns, however, were nibbling at the leaves without a care in the world.

Ah, the innocence of childhood.

"We didn't have deer in the city either," I said.

Teeny smiled wide. "Oh my goodness. Look at those

babies. Chelsea go crawl up next to them and pretend to be a baby deer."

Miss May laughed. "Now that I would like to see. Chelsea, go eat the leaves! They look tasty."

"A little salt and I'll eat anything," I said. "Or maybe some hot sauce? Still have that bottle in your purse, Teeny?"

Miss May laughed. Teeny joined in and the deer skittered away.

"You guys! Your laughter at my expense scared them away," I said.

"You should rejoice," Miss May said. "More leaves for you."

Teeny slapped her knee. Miss May doubled over. I crossed my arms, tiring of their charade. Then I spotted something moving a little further up the path.

"Shhhhhh!" I said. But they kept laughing. I pulled at Miss May's sleeve and pointed. "Be quiet. I think there's more wildlife."

Miss May covered her mouth. "That's a coyote."

Teeny stopped laughing. She turned white. "That's a whole herd of coyotes."

I gulped. "The correct term is pack."

22

FOREST FORTRESS

*E*ight large, wiry coyotes huddled together five feet up the hill. The canines were malnourished yet beautiful. Like runway models, but more deadly.

The alpha male bared his teeth in a warning snarl. My eyes widened. Although Miss May and I had investigated several murders in the prior year, that moment was the most scared I had been since moving back to Pine Grove. The depth of my nature and wildlife knowledge didn't help. My mind raced through coyote facts...

- Coyotes do not attack humans often. But they have.

- A single coyote has the potential to kill much larger prey with its powerful jaw.

- Although one coyote by his or herself isn't much to fear, a group of coyotes could be dangerous if threatened.

. . .

I also knew that when faced with a coyote the best course of action was to throw sticks and stones to scare them away. Unfortunately, at that moment my fear paralyzed me. And it looked like Teeny and Miss May were also frozen by fear because neither moved.

Teeny spoke through clenched teeth, "Should we call animal control?"

"I don't know," I whispered, also through clenched teeth. "But coyotes are usually diurnal or nocturnal hunters, so it is odd for them to be roaming around like this in daylight. They must be extremely hungry. Or something else is wrong."

"Oh my goodness, speak English, Chelsea," Teeny said.

"It doesn't matter anyway," Miss May said. She barely moved her lips at all as she spoke, and I had the thought that she'd be the best ventriloquist among us. "There's no phone service up here."

"That's great," Teeny muttered. "Comforting."

We fell quiet again, handing our fates over to, well, fate.

.   .   .

After about sixty seconds the alpha broke his stare and stalked into the brush as if nothing had happened. The other coyotes followed, breaking off one by one to fall in line behind Snarly McSnarlson.

Once the last of the animals disappeared into the brush, Miss May exhaled. So did I. And so did Teeny. Then we pressed forward, continuing our silent march through the forest.

Fifteen minutes later, we found ourselves outside an abandoned cabin at the top of the hill.

The cabin was a single story, single room house that had seen better days. Heck, it had probably seen better centuries. The siding was made of long wooden planks. The roof had fallen off, but for three sad shingles. A half-collapsed chimney rose along the left side like a gnarled finger.

A crumbling doorway and a broken window revealed snapshots of an equally shabby interior.

Next to the cabin, a toppled 1950s refrigerator was splayed like a wildebeest corpse, racks jutting like ribs from the rusted out remains. And the quiet sounds of a raven's wings overhead provided an eerie soundtrack to the scene.

· · ·

I gulped. "I don't think I believe in ghosts, but does anyone else feel like this place is haunted?"

"Oh this place is crawling with spirits," Teeny said. "Look at the chimney! That thing has 'ghost portal' written all over it."

Miss May turned to us. "You two stop. This place isn't haunted. But I think it might be where Wallace lives."

"I hope it's not where we die," I said.

Miss May took a step toward the cabin. "Hello? Anybody home?"

No answer. Miss May stepped through the doorway. I followed but Teeny lingered outside. "I'll hang out here. Stand guard. Avoid the ghosts."

"Whatever you want, T," Miss May said. "Holler if you need us."

Once through the door, I witnessed an absolute horror of interior design. *Or should I say interior resign?*

.   .   .

The dirt floors were dusty and uneven. Old records and newspapers were strewn everywhere. And a hammock suspended from the ceiling formed a makeshift bed.

Miss May took careful steps as she surveyed the perimeter of the room. "Wallace has been staying here. That's a fact."

"How do you know?" I asked.

"For starters, that's a new hammock. Can't be more than a few months old." She picked up a can of food off the floor. "And this empty can of black beans smells like beans, not rotted maggot trash."

"OK. Those are good clues. But how do you know it's Wallace?"

"I suppose it could be anyone. But we saw him walking in this direction. So... if it quacks like a duck..."

I nodded. She had a point. "So what do we do now?"

"Leave?" Teeny called from outside.

"No," Miss May said. "We look for clues. If Wallace

committed that murder, there's evidence in this room. And if he burglarized anyone in town, there should be evidence of that too."

"I don't see any of the stuff that was stolen from the bakeshop. None of the other junk looks stolen either. Unless you count taking stuff out of the trash as stealing."

"Legally, yes. Morally, no," Miss May said.

Teeny poked her head inside the cabin. "Hey. What's going on in here? Need to borrow my hot sauce? Blind a ghost in the face?"

"Why don't you come in and find out?" Miss May asked.

Teeny shook her head. "I don't do haunted cabins. Just let me know if you need the sauce."

Miss May shook her head with a small chuckle. I doubled down on the mission and did a second inspection of the ramshackle shack.

Much of the debris seemed to be left over from when a family lived there. There was a Christmas sing-along record from the 1950's. There was a porcelain doll with vacant eyes, missing an arm. And there was a yellowed newspaper dated from 1953.

I squatted down to sift through some artifacts and noticed that the floors weren't dirt after all. Beneath layers of caked-on mud, there were actually thick, oak planks. "These were beautiful floors once," I said.

Miss May grunted a reply. She was too interested in sifting through her own pile of detritus to pay much attention to the floors.

"I mean, like really beautiful," I said. "These were not standard for the time. This wood was brought in special. Is that not odd for a little house like this?"

"Sure, it's a fun interior design fact," Miss May said. "But I don't think it tells us too much about Wallace. Keep your eyes open for actual clues."

I moved more debris away and cleared a large swath of floor. "I think I'm onto something," I said. I didn't totally think I was onto anything, but I wanted to prove my aunt wrong for once. I pushed even more junk and dirt away, and then more. And within thirty seconds I had a five foot by five-foot swath of floor clear of debris.

. . .

I stood up to get a bird's-eye view. *Or, I guess a human's eye view, in that scenario.*

I felt a thrill of pleasure. The nice oak planks only covered a tiny portion of the cabin floor. The wood was not original to the house.

"The oak doesn't match the rest of the floor," I said. "See?"

"So the previous owners did some renovations," Miss May said.

"I don't think that's it," I said. I got back on my hands and knees and ran my fingers along the wood. And that's when I felt it. A few of the panels were slightly uneven, but only by a few millimeters.

"I think this is a trapdoor," I said. "Is there a crowbar or something around?"

Miss May grabbed a fire iron from the fireplace and handed it to me. "Now I'm interested."

I shoved the fire iron under the patch of floorboards and pried. Sure enough, the floorboards swung up and opened like a door, revealing a dark basement below.

. . .

I looked over at Miss May. "My interior design always comes in handy. Doesn't it?"

"It does." Miss May held up her hands and bowed her head. "Mea culpa."

"I accept your apology," I said.

"It wasn't exactly an apology, but OK." Miss May leaned over the trapdoor and looked down into the basement. "Who's going first? You or me?"

I thought back to Master Skinner's instructions and swallowed down my fear. "I'll go first."

Miss May nodded. "OK. Don't have too much fun."

I tried to smile, then swung my legs into the hole.

Each step of the rickety ladder into the weird cellar creaked as I climbed down. A wretched stench wafted upward, and I resisted the urge to hold my nose. The hole went much deeper than I expected. I jumped off the last one or two rungs of the ladder and landed with a soft thud.

. . .

Miss May descended the ladder behind me, flipping on the flashlight on her phone and shining it around the small, damp room.

The room was stacked with stolen goods. Along the far wall, I spotted all the stuff that had gone missing from the bakeshop. A mixer. A vintage sign. A wad of cash splashed on the floor.

Along another wall were boxes of rotting produce. I assumed those were the stolen goods from Petey's restaurant.

Cluttered in the middle of the room were computer monitors from the town library.

Then there were lawn gnomes. Birdhouses. Mailboxes. *You name it, Wallace had stolen it and hoarded it in his creepy little basement.*

"Look at all this stuff," I said. "This guy has been way busier than we thought."

"You're telling me," Miss May said. "Half this stuff is from the library. I didn't even know the library had been broken into."

"These are old monitors," I said. "Probably from storage. Maybe the librarians don't even know it yet."

Miss May shook her head. "Or maybe Chief Flanagan is keeping people quiet on the mayor's orders. Anything to protect Pine Grove's image as a Top 10 Destination for Bed and Breakfasts."

"And look at the stuff from the bake shop," I said. "It looks so sad down here. And it doesn't seem like he's tried to sell anything. It's all gathering dust and worms and cellar slime."

Miss May took me by the arm. "OK. Keep it down. Remember. This guy could be dangerous. We know he's a thief. That makes it even more likely that he's also the killer. And he could be lurking anywhere. "

Thud. Thud. Thud.

Boots pounded on the floor above us. Then someone shined a powerful flashlight down into the basement.

. . .

"Who's down there? Let me see your hands!"

Miss May shot me a nervous glance. "That doesn't sound like Wallace."

I shook my head.

Click-click. The unmistakable sound of someone loading a gun.

"I said let me see your hands!"

23

A SURPRISE VISITOR

*W*hen Miss May and I emerged from the basement, we were face to gun with a large, imposing man. He looked to be about fifty, he wore all black, and he had his hair pulled back in a ponytail. When the man spoke, he had a thick, Bronx accent.

"Who are you and what are you doing here?" The man kept his gun trained on us as he spoke.

Miss May held up her hands, palms out. "We're friends of Wallace. Up here looking for him."

The imposing man narrowed his eyes. "Wallace doesn't have friends."

Miss May let out a nervous chuckle. "Are you telling me you're not here on a friendly visit?"

The man reached into his pocket and pulled out a badge without moving his gun. He flapped the badge open. "James Johnson. Parole officer. NYPD."

Miss May and I exchanged a nervous glance.

"Did Wallace have a history of arrests in New York?" I asked.

"He got arrested once every couple of months for twenty years. For petty stuff. But who's counting?"

"Any chance you'd be willing to lower the weapon?" Miss May asked. "I'm an old lady. I could drop dead at the mere hint of danger. We're no threat to you. I'm sure you can see that."

Officer Johnson lowered his gun one inch at a time. "Fine. But no sudden movements."

Miss May laughed. "I couldn't make a sudden movement if my life depended on it. Knees. Hips. Ankles. You get it. Like I said, I'm old."

"And I'm clumsy," I said. "In case you were wondering."

Johnson looked from me, then back to Miss May. "You two are strange. I'm picking up on that now. An odd duo of some kind."

"If you want to know a secret about who we are," Miss May said. "I'll tell you."

"Everyone likes a secret," Johnson said.

"We're amateur sleuths. Wallace is a suspect in a murder that occurred down in Pine Grove a few days ago. We want to ask him some questions."

"You said he had committed a lot of crimes in the city? Do you think he could have killed?" I asked.

"Nah," Johnson said. "The guy is a little opossum. Ugly. Not fun to be around. But mostly a gentle offender."

Miss May exhaled a sigh of relief. "Great. So... Not a killer."

Johnson chuckled. "I didn't say that. He has a bit of a history with violence. Not murder. But listen, you met the guy. You tell me what you think."

"I think we need to find him. Fast. Do you know where he is?" Miss May asked.

"Does it look like I know where he is? My job is to know

where he is. And I'm standing in a little cabin up in the forest with an old lady and her clumsy sidekick."

"I'm assuming he missed a meeting with you?" Miss May asked.

"Your assumption would be correct," James said. "Not just one meeting, either. Several. Which is unlike him. Until a few weeks ago, Wallace was always on time for our little rendezvous."

"Until today," I said. "He had been hanging around Pine Grove."

"That's true," Miss May said. "But do you know where Wallace was prior to living in Pine Grove? We know about the affordable housing that got torn down on Waverly Place. But where did he go after that?"

"How do you know about all this crud?" Johnson put his hand back on his gun.

"Relax," Miss May said. "Like I said. We're sleuths."

"We also run an apple orchard and bake pies, cookies, and a delicious assortment of breads," I said. "At the *Thomas Family Fruit and Fir Farm,* anything is possible and everything is delicious."

"Are you advertising your business right now?" Johnson asked.

"I don't know what my niece is doing," Miss May said. "But I'm talking about Wallace. I want to know his history. Is he a threat to the people in Pine Grove? Is it possible he's lurking in this forest as we speak, hunting for a new victim?"

"If he's looking for a new victim, he'd be back in town. It's not like he knew we were coming up here," I said.

"You know what I mean, Chelsea," Miss May said.

Johnson groaned. "Enough already! You two are giving

me a migraine headache the size of the Sistine Chapel. I don't have time for this."

"Weird metaphor," I said.

"Whatever." James handed us his business card and started back down the hill. "If you see Wallace tell him I was here."

"I thought it was your job to find him," Miss May called.

Johnson turned back. "It's his job to be on time for our meetings. Next time I see him, I'm arresting him."

Miss May and I watched James Johnson disappear down the hill. That guy had more swagger in his ponytail than most people had in their entire bodies.

"Be careful," I called out. "There's a pack of coyotes on the loose."

James took his gun out of his holster and waved it in the air. "I'll be fine, ladies. Bye now."

A few seconds later, Teeny poked her head out from behind a tree. "Is he gone?"

I clutched my chest and stumbled back. I had totally forgotten Teeny had come with us to the cabin and her presence shocked me.

"Teeny! You scared me," I said. "Were you hiding behind a tree this whole time?"

Teeny nodded. "Big, scary guy comes up the hill, gun on his belt, what would you do?"

Miss May nodded. "You were smart to hide. That guy may not have been evil, but he was not a good conversationalist."

Teeny wiped a chunk of tree bark off her shirt. "Can you girls believe that Wallace fella is such a crook?"

"I can," I said.

"Me too," said Miss May.

"I guess that's true," Teeny said. "He did seem a lot like a crook. But what does that mean? What do we do now?"

Miss May looked around. All was quiet. "What can we do? It's going to be dark soon. We should head back to town."

I threw up my hands in protest. "For real? We just discovered a trove of hidden treasure in the cabin."

"Maybe we can tell the cops," Teeny said.

"Chief Flanagan won't do anything," I said. "We need to return the stolen stuff to its owners."

Miss May chuckled. "I appreciate your Lady Robin Hood mentality. And I agree. Flanagan is a horrible, no good, very bad chief. But if we move those stolen goods or report them, Wallace will know we're onto him. And the last thing we want is to alert a killer to our presence."

"So you really think Wallace is the killer?" Teeny asked.

Miss May shrugged. "He's our best suspect."

"But why go back to town to find him?" Teeny said. "We're already up at his secret lair. Let's wait in the shadows and attack when he returns home, dragging the body of his new victim by the pinky toes."

"Teeny!" I said.

"OK, dragging them by the big toes, then. Is that anatomically correct enough, Chels?"

I shook my head. I just wanted Teeny to stop talking about dragging corpses by their foot digits.

"Better idea," Miss May said. "Let's be proactive and find Wallace before he kills his next victim. Two birds, one stone."

"I guess that makes sense," Teeny said. "And I suppose my hot sauce may not be super effective against a crazed murderer determined to kill no matter the cost."

"At last you admit it," Miss May said. "Hot sauce is not a weapon."

"Next time I'll bring spicy mustard," Teeny said. "That'll get him."

Miss May shook her head.

"So now we head back to town?" I asked. "Try to drum up more info on where Wallace might be?"

Miss May nodded. "Maybe we can stop for dinner first. Then continue the search."

"Works for me," Teeny said. "I'm hungry! How about chocolate chip cookies for an appetizer, and ice cream for the main course?"

I chuckled. Teeny was never one to shy away from dessert for dinner. I liked that about her. But my stomach twisted into a tight coil at the thought of food.

A coyote yapped in the distance and I started down the hill. I may not have been hungry, but I wasn't in the mood to be eaten, either.

24

LOST AND FOUND

*O*ur walk back toward town began with excited chatter between Teeny and Miss May about ice cream flavors and toppings.

But as evening crept closer, the sun waved its slow good-bye, and the forest transformed from a lush green wonderland into a shadowy creep-fest. Like a landscape straight from the minds of the brothers Grimm.

I had a bad feeling.

Before long, Miss May and Teeny had caught my bad feeling. Tensions were rising. And none of us seemed to remember how to get out of the forest.

At first, Miss May suggested we follow the path back the way we came. That made sense, so Teeny and I agreed. But then we came to a fork in the path we had not noticed on our journey toward the cabin. Miss May insisted she knew the right way. Then we came to another fork in the road and she admitted that she felt lost.

As soon as Miss May uttered the word "lost," my heart sank.

Growing up, Miss May and I had gotten lost many times.

She was a proud woman. Often too proud to admit when she didn't know what she was doing. So whenever she did admit a mistake... there was a problem.

"I can't be lost!" Teeny said. "I'm too hungry for that. And I'm too scared. This forest is full of trolls!"

"Trolls?" I said.

Teeny gave me a dirty look.

I shrugged. "I'm sorry. But I don't think trolls are our number one concern."

"They are!" Teeny insisted.

"But are they?"

"You're telling me, if you saw a troll right now, that wouldn't be your number one concern?"

"I mean, I guess, but there are no trolls here!"

"Ladies!" Miss May said. "We can't turn on each other right now. We're three smart, resourceful women. Chelsea, you went to Duke for goodness sakes. We need to put our heads together and find our way out of here."

It's not like I studied cartography, I thought. But even so, I wanted to help. I looked around to try to determine which way we should walk. I pointed at the fading sun. "OK. The sun is going that way. So what does that mean?"

Teeny huffed. "The sun rises in the west and sets in the east, Chelsea."

"The sun rises in the east!" I snipped.

"It does not," Teeny said. "You wouldn't know the sun if it bit you in the face."

I turned to Miss May. So did Teeny. My aunt winced. "I think Chelsea's right but I'm not sure. Ugh. I'm terrible with directions!"

Teeny balled up her fists. "You're not allowed to be terrible with directions! You insisted you knew the right direction!"

"I thought I did," Miss May said. "But now everything looks like...trees."

"I don't understand how we got so lost," I said. "We walked straight up the hill. Doesn't it follow that to get home all we needed to do was walk straight down the hill?"

"The hill went up, then the hill went down, then the hill went up again. It's the hill's fault!" Teeny said.

"OK," Miss May said, "let's calm down and use our heads. The hills surrounding Pine Grove are pure nature in every direction except toward town. So maybe we can listen for traffic or something. And walk toward the sound."

I exhaled. Finally a good idea. "OK. Let's listen."

We closed our eyes and listened for traffic. The only problem was that it was almost 7 PM. By that time most people had deserted Pine Grove. So we needed to focus if we wanted to hear anything.

After a few seconds, Miss May opened her eyes. "Do you hear that?"

I shrugged. So did Teeny.

"I think it's the sound of a lawnmower. Hear the growling? Didn't the town just buy two mowers for that overgrown baseball field near Brook Road?"

"Oh yeah," I said. "You're right. I think I hear it."

Miss May walked toward the sound of the lawnmowers. Teeny and I followed.

We walked for a few more minutes but somehow the sound got further away. A raven cawed and swooped right across our path. The wildlife of the Pine Grove woods was really spooking up my vibes today.

As the sun finally set, and we slipped into a gray dusk, my chest tightened. And my head swirled with nightmarish images of the three of us, growing long beards and sucking sap from trees for sustenance.

"Miss May... What do we do if we're actually lost?" I said. "I don't wanna suck a tree!"

"Well we have no phone service." Miss May shrugged. "Maybe we huddle together for warmth?"

"I call cream!" Teeny said.

"What does that mean, 'cream'?" I asked.

"If we're making a human Oreo, I want to be the cream. That way I get maximum warmth."

Oh boy. This was getting desperate.

"It's not that weird," Teeny said. "You girls have more built-in cream. I need the extra flubber."

I laughed. "That is so rude!"

"Is not," Teeny said. "I love your flubber. That flubber is what's gonna keep you from dying in the woods!"

"Quit saying flubber!" Miss May pointed in a new direction. "This way. Follow me."

"You know where you're going now?" I asked.

"Yup," Miss May said. "I'm walking a thousand steps straight in that direction. No more zigging and zagging. Just a straight line. OK?"

"Works for me," Teeny said.

"Works for me too," I said.

"Good. I'll count." Miss May counted her steps aloud as she walked and Teeny and I followed behind.

But right around step number ten, Miss May tripped over a log, lost her footing and took a tumble...right down the side of a hill.

Teeny and I tripped over the same log and fell down the hill after her. And the resulting thump-thump to the bottom was not pretty.

I tried to grab a tree branch to slow my fall. It cut my hand and I kept tumbling. I rolled over a boulder, which caught me in the ribs with a sickening crunk. I clawed at the ground with desperation, but to no avail.

I didn't stop moving until I got the bottom of the hill.

Crunch. Thud. "Ouch."

Right on top of Miss May.

Thank goodness for that extra flubber, I thought.

Teeny rolled to a stop a few feet beside me, cursing under her breath. And the three of us spent the next ten seconds groaning. Then I sat up and winced, rubbing my arm.

"Is everyone OK?" I asked.

Teeny pulled herself up beside me. "I'm all right."

"I'm OK too," Miss May said. "But he's not."

Miss May gestured behind me. I turned.

And there was Wallace the Traveler...

...impaled on a stick.

Dead.

25

KILLED AND KEBABBED

*D*iscovering Wallace, skewered as he was, I felt the same way I always did upon discovering a body. Devastated. Sad. And no longer hungry.

Wallace had been such an intimidating presence on the streets of Pine Grove. Angry. Yelling. Unpredictable. All that rage and recklessness had somehow distanced me from the vulnerability behind it. But in so many ways, Wallace had been a childlike presence around town. He had spoken his mind. He had expressed his emotions. And he'd danced like no one was watching even though everyone was.

That day in the forest, his vulnerability was all I saw. *Dying is the ultimate vulnerability*, I thought. But it was more than Wallace's particular predicament, his eyes looked so helpless.

Teeny's lip quivered. "We're so lucky we survived that fall. If we had landed like he did…"

Miss May inhaled through her nose. "He didn't land like this. Look at the angle of the stick. He was…"

"Kebabbed?" I said.

"That's a horrifying way of putting it, but yes," Miss May said.

I looked a few feet away from Wallace's corpse and I couldn't believe my eyes.

"Miss May, look! It's Rosenberg's briefcase!"

Indeed, there was the briefcase, wedged in a nearby bush.

I limped over and picked the case up. When I grabbed it, the briefcase flopped open and several folders and papers spilled out.

Miss May hurried over. "The fall broke the lock?"

"Or someone else did," I said. "Maybe Wallace figured out how to open it."

Miss May shook her head. "And KP said it wasn't possible."

A coyote yowled in the distance and my arms tightened. I remembered we were lost in the woods, with at least eight coyotes nearby.

"Uh-oh," I said.

Miss May looked over at me. "What?"

"I forgot. Coyotes can be carrion-feeders."

"What does that mean?" Miss May asked.

I gulped. "If they're hungry, they'll eat almost anything. Including um, dead things."

"I'm not worried about that," Miss May said. "I'm more concerned there's a killer on the loose. And they could be hiding anywhere."

"We should go," I said. "Now."

Miss May nodded. But Teeny couldn't seem to tear her eyes away from the body.

I had forgotten, Teeny hadn't come face-to-face with as many murder victims as Miss May and I had.

"I feel like we should say something," Teeny said. "A few words for the deceased."

Miss May nodded. "OK. Chelsea, you can do it."

"Why do I have to do it?" I asked.

"Will you just talk?" Miss May glared.

"OK. Fine." I took a deep breath. "Let's see. Wallace, we didn't know you well. And it seems like life might have dealt you a rough hand. But you danced with grace, and you moved through the world on your own terms. That's the noblest way anyone can live. And I'll miss seeing you in Pine Grove."

"Amen," Teeny said.

We bowed our heads in a spontaneous gesture of respect. Then Miss May started away.

"Hold on a second!" I said.

Miss May turned back. "What?"

"The briefcase!" I said.

Miss May shook her head. "Oh my goodness. All right. Gather it up and let's go."

"Give me two seconds." I tried to read the documents as I scooped them into the broken briefcase. But it was too dark.

I turned back to Miss May. "We're keeping these, right? We can read them later?"

Miss May nodded. "I think we should report Wallace's death to the police. But yeah... There's no way we're turning those papers over to the cops before we get a look at them."

"Don't turn them over ever," Teeny said. "That corrupt chief will burn them in her fireplace without even reading!"

I shuffled the last document into the briefcase and squeezed it shut. "Got it. Let's go."

As dusk turned to night, the lights of Pine Grove twinkled, and we used them to guide us as we trudged back to town.

Once we stumbled out of the forest, we stashed the briefcase under some blankets in the back of Miss May's van, then headed toward the police department to report Wallace's death.

Flanagan crossed her arms as we entered the precinct. "Well. Look what the cat vomited on the carpet. What do you three want?"

Miss May told Flanagan about Wallace. Flanagan rolled her eyes and scoffed throughout.

Then, once Miss May stopped talking, Flanagan spoke with a cold and impersonal tone. "Thanks for the information, ladies. I'll let the coroner's office know. And I'll send Officer Hercules over to check out the scene."

"Hercules!" I cried. "He can barely answer the phones without tripping over his own feet!"

Scrawny little Hercules looked up from a game of solitaire at the reception desk. "Hey! I heard that."

"No offense, Hercules. I just think a kebabbed man in the forest deserves multiple officers. I know that sounds harsh, but it's just true."

"Miss Thomas, please," Flanagan said. "Control your babbling fits."

"I wasn't even babbling!" I said.

"You were about to," Flanagan said. "And we have police work to do. Did you not say you, your aunt, and Tiny rolled down the hill where you found the deceased?"

"Yes, but—"

"So is it not possible, nay, likely, that the deceased also fell down that hill and was, as you said, 'kebabbed' in the process?"

I huffed. "That kebabbing was no accident!"

Hercules piped up, "I'm sorry, I feel it's a little insensitive to talk about a dead man like he's Greek meat."

"No one asked you, Hercules," Chief Flanagan snapped. "Now if you'll excuse me—"

Miss May stepped forward. "This is a suspicious death, Flanagan. You need to investigate."

"Thanks for your input, apple lady. But I'm the Chief of Police. I will go through the proper channels and I will show respect for the dead. What I will not do, however, is show respect for you. Or your niece. Or Teeny Weeny. Why is she eating ice cream in my department?"

Teeny looked up from an ice cream cone she was eating. "My name is Teeny, no Weeny. And this is my dinner. And that was a murder up there!"

Flanagan chuckled. "You ladies don't seem to understand. Accidental deaths are common in small communities like ours. Not murders. I'm sick of you and your niece changing that perception, damaging Pine Grove's reputation, and wasting everyone's time and tax money."

"Every case we've solved was an actual murder," Miss May said. "You would know that if your department had done anything to help."

Flanagan held the door open for us to leave. "I'll take it from here, ladies. Don't let the door hit your ice cream on the way out."

Flanagan's cavalier attitude was not acceptable. So I took a stand.

"No! You can't just shut us down like that," I said. "There's something going on in Pine Grove. Someone else could get hurt."

"I'll be sure to educate the public about the dangers of hiking without proper preparation," Flanagan said. "No one should go into those woods without a map and rations. Or you're right. Someone could get hurt."

Hercules snickered.

"Stop laughing Hercules," I said. "You think it's funny that you work for what the French call, 'les incompétents'? Where's Wayne? He'll believe me."

Flanagan got in my face. "You will not use French to disparage my name in this department!"

I glared at Flanagan. "Do you even speak French? Maybe that was a compliment."

"You're about to cross a line, Miss Thomas," Flanagan warned.

Miss May took me by the arm. "Let's go, Chels. We've got a crime to solve."

26

PAIN IN THE WAYNE

$\mathcal{M}$iss May reprimanded me as soon as we stepped outside. "Chelsea. What are you doing, confronting the chief of police like that?"

I balled up my fists. "I'm sorry but I hate when people in power just turn a blind eye to justice. It's not right. That lady is ridiculous!"

"Chelsea!" Miss May said in a hushed tone. "We're still at the precinct."

"OK," I said. "I'll simmer down. But that woman does not deserve to be Chief of Police."

Teeny took a big lick of her ice cream. "Word up to that."

Miss May turned on Teeny. "Please don't encourage her. This is serious."

"It is serious," I said. "And Flanagan's not doing anything about it!"

Miss May exhaled. "Chelsea. We're never going to find the killer if we get locked up before the criminal does."

"She's got a good point." A deep voice boomed from nearby.

Wayne closed the door on his squad car and approached. "Are you OK, Chelsea?"

"No," I said. "I'm riled up."

"I can't have this conversation anymore," Miss May said. "Wayne. Will you please talk sense into this girl?" She turned to me. "We'll be in the car."

Miss May charged toward her yellow VW van but Teeny did not follow. "Teeny. Come on," Miss May said.

Teeny hesitated. "But I want to listen. They might get flirty."

Miss May shook her head, "Not if we're standing around eavesdropping!"

Teeny took a big lick of her ice cream cone. "Fine." She tailed after Miss May to the van.

Then, once again...I found myself alone with Detective Wayne Hudson.

"So what's going on?" he asked.

I looked down. "I got a little frustrated. I'm fine."

Wayne chuckled. "I get it. Flanagan can be... difficult."

I nodded. "Yeah. And this investigation is stressing me out. So... I guess I lost it in there."

"What's going on?"

I looked up at Wayne. He looked kind. And concerned. So I spewed the facts of the case all over him.

The suspects, the cabin in the woods, the parole officer. I told him about discovering Wallace's body and my inappropriate use of the word kebab as a murder verb.

Wayne kept his head down the whole time, listening. When I stopped to catch my breath, he put his hand on my arm. It was a comforting gesture, and I relaxed a little.

"Maybe you and your aunt should take a backseat on this one," he said. "Let us figure it out."

I pushed his hand away. "Are you serious? We're the only

ones who are doing anything to find the killer. Flanagan thinks the kebabbing is just a coincidence!"

"You really should not use the word kebab that way," Wayne said. "But yes, I'm serious."

I scoffed.

"Don't laugh, it makes sense. Listen, I'm not saying I plan on turning all this over to Flanagan. If she deems Wallace's death an accident, fine. But I'll use department resources to find the truth on my own. So you don't have to. So you can stay out of danger."

I glared at Wayne. "I'm not a defenseless lamb, Wayne. And you're not in charge here. You haven't helped with this investigation. You had no idea Wallace was a suspect. And you don't even know about the briefcase!"

Wayne narrowed his eyes. "What briefcase?"

Good job, Chelsea. Way to spill the briefcase beans. Think of an excuse. Quick!

"No briefcase," I said. "I misspoke. I meant to say, coyotes. There were hungry coyotes in the woods. They could damage the crime scene. Did you know coyotes are diurnal?"

"You said 'briefcase' instead of 'coyotes'?" Wayne asked. "That's a stretch, even for you."

"OK. Fine. If you must know, it was a Freudian slip," I said. "I used the word 'briefcase' because someone gifted me a beautiful briefcase. And it was Germany Turtle. Yeah. He likes me. And I'm not sure what to do about that either."

That's what they call a deflection, ladies and gentlemen. Invent a love briefcase to take the attention away from a murder briefcase. Oldest trick in the book.

Wayne furrowed his brow. "That weird Turtle kid gave you a briefcase to tell you he has a crush on you?"

"It's a great briefcase," I said. "Vintage leather. And Germany's not weird. He's eccentric."

When in doubt, double down on your outrageous lie. And hey, if it makes a hunky detective jealous? Bonus points.

Wayne's walkie-talkie blared with a call about Wallace. He turned the volume down. "That's about your guy. Seems Flanagan might conduct an investigation, after all."

"Good," I said. "She should."

"I should go help," Wayne said.

"Go right ahead," I said. "Serve your fearless leader."

Wayne cocked his head. Thought about saying something. Then walked away.

I sighed. Our dance in the barn seemed like it had happened in a dream. *Or*, I thought, *was it a nightmare?*

That night, Miss May and I spread the contents of the briefcase across the kitchen table.

There were about a dozen documents in the pile but only a few seemed notable.

First, we found a ledger in which Rosenberg had documented every public official he had ever bribed.

The list did not include Chief Flanagan. *Disappointing.*

Mayor Delgado, however, had received several direct deposits from Rosenberg in the preceding months. And once Miss May tallied the sum of Delgado's bribes, we both staggered back from the papers in stunned disbelief.

"Three hundred thousand dollars," I said. "That's a small fortune."

Miss May nodded. "Yup. And Delgado has done a good job of hiding it. No new car. No fancy jewelry. Nothing."

"What's the point of accepting bribes if you don't spend the money?" I asked.

"I'm sure she'll spend it," Miss May said. "A little at a time. Once the attention dies down."

I sighed. "But does this give her a motive?"

"It could," Miss May said. "Maybe Rosenberg planned to cut off her payments, and that angered her? I'm not sure."

"But what about Wallace? How does this tie back to him?"

Miss May scratched her chin. Classic sleuth move. "Let's think... Wallace had the briefcase. And the briefcase contained information that could have sent the mayor to jail. So maybe the mayor killed him to get the information?"

"But the killer left the briefcase behind," I said.

"That's true," Miss May said. "Or he or she didn't have time to climb down the hill and gather the case and its contents. Maybe they heard us coming and had to hide. Remember it was almost dark when we found Wallace. And we didn't have an easy time getting down that hill."

I turned my attention back to the documents spread on the kitchen table.

"What else do we have here?"

Miss May sifted through the documents. "Nothing, nothing, nothing." She paused when she got to a large, tattered binder.

"What's this?"

Miss May flipped the binder open. "Old photos. Weird. A whole album."

She slid the binder to me. Sure enough, it contained pages upon pages of family photos.

"These are photos of the Rosenbergs," I said. "Look at this caption. 'Hank, 5th Birthday.'"

I flipped through the pages. More photos of Hank, his parents and his siblings. "Looks like he was the younger of two boys."

"That's odd. Usually the youngest kid in a family is the nicest," Miss May said.

"Is that true if you're an only child?" I batted my eyes, fishing for a compliment.

"Sure. But the oldest is the most spoiled. So you fit the bill on that one too."

I smiled. "I'll take it."

Miss May grabbed a manila envelope and slid the contents out. "Oh my."

I crossed behind her to get a look. "What?"

"Divorce papers."

"From his wife?!" I asked.

Miss May looked at me. "No. From his dog."

"OK. Stupid question. When did they file?"

Miss May's face whitened. "Two years ago. Susan signed. But not Hank."

I slid one last sheet of paper from the envelope. "Look. There's a cover letter. 'Hank. Sign the darn papers. Enough is enough. Susan.'"

I passed Miss May the letter, and she read it with wide eyes. "OK," she said. "So... There's some new motive with the wife."

I nodded. "In that theory Susan killed Hank because he wouldn't grant her a divorce?"

Miss May nodded. "The pending divorce would explain the separate rooms for everything."

"But she seemed so upset when Rosenberg died. In her own weird way. And she thought Master Skinner was the killer."

"That's true," Miss May said. "But maybe she was misdirecting us. Keeping us away from the real killer...herself."

"She never provided an alibi, did she?"

Miss May shook her head.

I sighed. If we had known the briefcase contained that many clues, we would have tried harder to get KP to wrestle it open.

"So what should we do next?" I asked.

"Honestly," Miss May looked at me over her glasses. "I want to know what Teeny thinks."

27

CHAINS AND CRANES

e woke up at 6 AM the next morning and headed to town to see Teeny. Both Miss May and I were too tired to talk. My aunt drove at a steady pace most of the way, but she stopped short when she caught sight of the Rosenberg building.

Someone had parked a construction crane out front, with a wrecking ball dangling from the arm. Arthur and Petunia had chained themselves to the front door, chanting.

"Is demolition set for today?" Miss May asked.

"I thought Monday," I said. "But there's the crane…"

Miss May rolled down the window so we could hear what Arthur and Petunia were chanting.

"Save our town! Save our town!"

I shrugged. "Not the most original chant I've heard, but it gets the point across."

Miss May honked and gestured for Arthur and Petunia to come talk.

Arthur called out, "We're chained to the building, May! What do you want?"

"What's going on? You're still protesting?"

Petunia pumped her fist. "Dang right we are, missy! We'll fight this thing to the bloody end!"

"It's only Saturday," Miss May said. "What's with the crane?"

Arthur shook his head. "It showed up under the cover of night, like a sneaky mechanical T-Rex." *Weird comparison*. "The construction crew started up the wrecking ball this morning!"

"So we broke out the chains!" Petunia pumped her fist in the air.

"We're doing all we can to save this building," Arthur said. "You're on our side, right?"

"You know I'm on your side," Miss May said.

"Good," Arthur said. "Rosenberg gave his life to ruin this town. And I'll give my life to protect it!"

"Have you called the cops?" Miss May asked.

Arthur laughed to himself. "Everyone's always asking about the police. Yes, we called them. They said they were on their way an hour ago. I'm still waiting."

"We called the mayor, too," Petunia said. "No answer. That scum sucker!"

"I doubt anybody is at work in town hall yet," I said.

"We didn't call town hall," Arthur said. "We called her house. I called fifteen times straight. Left fifteen messages, too. Petunia left a message just making noises. Bah-bah-bah-bah-bah. Like that but in a nice rhythm. She's very creative."

Petunia nodded. "I had fun with it, but the message was clear!"

Miss May and I exchanged a concerned look. Were Arthur and Petunia losing it?

"The only person who answered our calls was Sudeer." Arthur pointed across the street. "He came right down."

I looked across the street. Sure enough there was Sudeer, pacing back and forth with his smart phone to his ear.

"I've said horrible things to that guy," Petunia said. "And I'm not sorry about them! But he has proven to be less of a waste than I presumed."

Miss May forced a smile. "Sudeer is a nice guy. Cutest little babies too."

Arthur scoffed. "Nice guy? Yeah, right! He's still a traitor!"

Sudeer approached with a nervous smile.

"Miss May. Chelsea. Hi. Did I hear my name?"

"You heard the word traitor and got confused," Arthur said.

Miss May shot a warning look at Arthur. "We were just talking about your adorable babies."

Sudeer sighed. "It's been days since I've seen their faces. This project—"

"This project is despicable," Arthur said.

"Yeah!" Petunia added. "You sold your soul to the devil, Sudeer. I hope you got a pretty penny for it."

"Look," Sudeer said. "I'm doing my best. You know that. I just got off the phone with the president of the company. He agreed to delay the demolition until Monday."

"It was already delayed until Monday. Those cowards tried to sneak the wrecking ball in today. Not on our watch!" Arthur said. "We want the demolition cancelled!"

"I'm working on it. But for now the delay is the best I can do," Sudeer said. "My bosses are... challenging."

"How did you convince them to delay the demolition?" Miss May asked.

Sudeer sighed. "I told the board today was an Indian holiday and if they didn't let me take the day off, I would sue them and go on the news about how they are not tolerant of other cultures. They believed me. This is the one time I've been happy how little Americans know about my culture."

Arthur shouted. "Yes, three cheers for your ignorant bosses. Next time you talk to them, tell them that neither Petunia nor I will break these chains."

Sudeer nodded. "I'll let them know. Once I'm done celebrating 'Vishi-Vishi,' the sacred Indian day of resting your toes."

"Wow, that sounds super made-up," I said. "And I once made up a finance expert named Millini Gustafo."

"It does sound fake. But I think your toes could actually use some rest," Miss May put her hand on Sudeer's arm. "Those babies need their dad to catch up on his sleep."

Sudeer smiled a tired smile and trudged away.

Miss May turned back to Arthur and Petunia. "All right. You got two more days. Now do you two want to take the chains off and join us for breakfast?"

"Never!" Petunia said. "But will you get me a muffin?"

28

BODACIOUS BERRY BAKE

A few minutes later, we arrived at *Grandma's*. The place was quiet before the morning rush, and I relished the peaceful atmosphere.

The teenage girl who Teeny had hired to replace Petey vacuumed the main dining room. Someone had propped a mop against the front door. And the smell of cinnamon and vanilla swirled in the air.

A few seconds after we arrived, Teeny emerged from the kitchen wiping her hands on an apron. "There you two are! What happened? I thought you were coming bright and early."

"It's 6:45," Miss May said.

"Please! I'm on my fourth cup of coffee." Teeny pulled off her apron and tossed it behind the counter. "Come on. I've got something I want you to try."

Teeny grabbed Miss May by the hand and led us to our favorite booth. "That berry pie you made the other night inspired me so I whipped up a berry oatmeal bake I think people will love. If they don't love it, I'm kicking them out of the restaurant."

I laughed. Teeny was a wonderful hostess. But if guests criticized her cooking, her décor, the wait time, the service, the silverware, the napkin creases, the place mats... *You get the idea.* She didn't love criticism. She usually banned one customer from the restaurant each month, on average.

"Hold on a second," Miss May said. "The pie Rosenberg died on... inspired you?"

Teeny shrugged. "Not the literal pie of death. But yes. I thought it was one of your berry best. Get it. Berry?"

Miss May chuckled. "I get it, T. Clever."

We slid into the booth. Teeny sat opposite us and signaled to the vacuuming waitress. "We're ready, Annabeth!"

Annabeth, who wore her hair in her face and walked with an odd shuffle, hurried into the kitchen. Seconds later, she emerged with a casserole tray of Teeny's new creation and set it on our table along with plates and forks.

"Now presenting Teeny's magnificent berry bake it is a berry bake like no other please enjoy and let me know what else I can get you thank you so much."

Annabeth shuffled away, keeping her eyes on the ground.

Miss May cocked her head at Teeny. "New employee?"

"Annabeth. Friend of a friend. Real weird girl. She's coming along. But don't worry about her. Worry about this berry bake!"

Teeny gestured to the dish like Vanna White. "Ta-da! The every berry oatmeal bake of your dreams."

I leaned forward and sniffed. The aroma warmed my entire body. "Mmm. Brown sugar. Vanilla. And is that almond extract I smell?"

Teeny nodded. "You're teaching her well, May. Almond

extract it is. And you might not smell it, but there's about three refrigerators worth of unsalted butter in that thing."

"Just three refrigerators?" Miss May asked. "I use four refrigerators' worth in my piecrust."

Teeny and Miss May laughed. But I kept my focus trained on the berry bake. It looked and smelled so delicious my mouth watered.

Teeny chuckled. "Chelsea, don't take this the wrong way, but are you drooling like a wild dog?"

"What's the right way to take that?" I asked.

Teeny shrugged and I wiped the saliva from my mouth. "Anyway, it's not my fault you made me drool. You baked this delicious creation and now you're taunting us with it!"

"Point taken!" Teeny served each of us a heaping helping and handed us forks.

I took a bite and widened my eyes. "How does this taste even better than it smells?"

"Could be the three refrigerators of butter," Miss May said, mouthful of berry bake. "But oh my this is scrumptious!"

Teeny clapped her hands. "Great! So it's on the menu. But what should we call it?"

"I thought you had already named it berry oatmeal bake of your dreams or whatever," I said.

Teeny looked disgusted. "That's not the name. That's a bare-bones description of the dish. I need something clever. Chelsea, use your college brain."

I laughed. "How about the Bodacious Berry Bake?"

Teeny snapped her fingers. "Triple alliteration! I'm drowning in how cute that is. Please. Save me! Throw me a flotation device made of berry bake!"

We spent the next few minutes devouring the Bodacious

Berry Bake, then Miss May filled Teeny in on the investigation.

Once all was said, done, and devoured, Teeny summed things up. "So Wallace is dead. And the mystery briefcase contained a photo album, divorce papers, and evidence that Rosenberg bribed the mayor."

Miss May nodded. "So our quandary is... who do we question first?"

"I suppose you don't want me to suggest something I learned on North Port Diaries?" Teeny asked.

Miss May smirked. "That's correct."

"Then it's easy," Teeny said. "You need to talk to the mayor."

"Is it that obvious?" Miss May asked. "We also learned Susan Rosenberg wanted a divorce."

"But only the mayor would have had the motive to kill both Rosenberg and Wallace," Teeny said.

Miss May took a bite of Berry Bake. "It's possible that there were two different killers in this case."

"I agree," Teeny said. "And if it turns out the mayor is innocent, we should pursue that theory. But time is of the essence, here. So why not start with the suspect who could be culpable in both murders?"

Miss May looked impressed. "Whoa. Teeny. That's... that's an amazing point."

Teeny smiled. "Guess what?"

"What?" Miss May asked.

"I saw it on an episode of North Port Diaries."

Miss May and I laughed.

"You are too much!" I said.

Teeny shrugged.

"But can we back up one second," I said. "I want to make sure I understand."

"Sure," said Teeny. "I've seen the episode two dozen times."

"Our working theory is that Mayor Delgado killed both victims. She murdered Hank because he controlled her with bribes and she wanted an out. And she murdered Wallace because he had evidence of the bribes and she wanted to keep her corruption a secret."

"And bingo was her name-o," said Teeny.

"It's also possible Susan killed Rosenberg," I said. "Because she wanted a divorce."

"And it's possible Wallace killed Rosenberg," Miss May said, patiently going over the theory. "Because Rosenberg destroyed Wallace's Section 8 housing."

"But we're not pursuing those leads because we have limited time. So we're focusing on the suspect who had the motive to kill both victims."

"That's how it goes in *North Port Diaries*," Teeny said.

"What happens at the end of that episode?" I asked.

Teeny cringed. "You really want me to tell you?"

I nodded.

"The detectives all die."

29

MAYOR, MAY I?

*W*hen we walked up to town hall, it was still before 8 AM, and there were no cars in the parking lot.

"It looks like the mayor's not at work yet," Miss May said.

Teeny scoffed. "That figures. Government employees never arrive before 9 AM and they never stay after 5 PM. Except for government gravediggers. They work the same hours though. Just in reverse."

I looked over at Teeny. "I don't think government gravedigger is a real job."

Teeny shrugged. "Could be."

"Yoo-hoo!"

We turned to see Deb walking toward us with her Persian cat, Sandra Day O'Connor, on a leash. Deb greeted us with a smile and brimmed with happy energy. But then Miss May turned the conversation to Sandra's quest for love, and Deb's face fell.

"My heart breaks for Sandra," Deb said. "Still single, after all my hard work and effort. Although I'm sure you'd agree she's the most beautiful feline in Pine Grove."

Ummmmm, sure?

Deb's voice wavered. "I tell Sandra there are no eligible bachelors in this town and that she's better off alone. But at night, once the day slows down, she gets lonely. And I understand that. Hence my search for her suitor."

Miss May nodded. "I get it. Sandra deserves a life partner like the rest of us."

"What about that feral tomcat that hangs out under the dumpster over by *Ewing's Eats?*" Teeny asked. "That fella seems friendly, for a stray."

Deb glared. "My Sandra will not be seen with a dumpster cat. Not that there's anything wrong with strays. But he and Sandra would have nothing to meow about."

I chuckled.

Deb turned on me. "This is serious, Chelsea. You know what it's like to be young and alone."

My jaw dropped. "Hey. I'm not alone."

Miss May chuckled. "She's not that young, either."

"Yes I am!" I said. "I'm hot and young and I have multiple suitors! I'm playing the field."

"Also, Sandra has never been in a serious relationship," Teeny said. "Chelsea was almost married."

"We all know how that turned out," Deb said.

Sandra tugged on her leash. Probably Sandra was embarrassed and wanted to go home. *Or maybe that's just me*, I thought.

Deb kneeled beside the cat. "Okay sweetheart. We're going." She stood up once more. "If you meet any handsome tomcats—"

"We'll call," said Miss May. "Right away."

A few minutes later, the mayor's car pulled into the lot and Mayor Delgado climbed out. She wore an impeccable pant-suit, as always. Her heels clacked as she climbed the steps toward the main entrance.

"Morning, Linda!" Miss May called out.

The mayor slowed her pace when she saw us. "Ladies. How can I help you?"

Miss May waved the mayor away. "Oh! We don't need help. We were just taking a morning walk."

"Morning walks are part of our routine now," I said. "It's part of our new healthy lifestyle for healthy living and being healthy and eating superfoods. Açaí. Is that how you say it? Ah-sigh-eeeeee?"

Miss May looked at me like I was crazy. Then she looked back to the mayor. "Yes. What Chelsea said. But with fewer words. Anyway, how are you?"

"I'm fine, May. But I have a busy day and I need to—"

"Cut the bull, Delgado." Teeny stepped forward. "You know why we're here. We want to talk about Rosenberg."

The mayor offered a tight smile. "As I told Miss May, I only answer questions from official members of the press, not random folks on bizarre 'health walks' nowhere near their homes."

"Every journey starts with one step," I said. "People on the *Today Show* are always saying that."

The mayor stepped past us and reached for the door but Teeny blocked her path, "Look at you!" Teeny said. "One mention of Rosenberg, and you're quaking in your sensible heels. Sweating through your pant suit. Hit her with the goods, May!"

Miss May spoke to Teeny through gritted teeth. "Teeny. What are you doing?"

Teeny responded with oblivious enthusiasm. "I'm recreating the episode of *North Port Diaries*. I thought that's what you wanted."

Mayor Delgado crossed her arms. "You two know I can hear you, right?"

"They're just being silly," I said, trying to smooth the tension. "Babbling. You know about babbling, right? He babbles. She babbles. Everyone goes babble babble. I'm doing it now!"

Teeny shook her head. "It's too late for that, Chelsea. We need to stick it to Mayor Linda or she's going to get away."

"Teeny! Stop!" Miss May glared.

"No, May! In *North Port Diaries*, the sleuths go for the jugular!" *The sleuths who end up dead, you mean?* Teeny got right in the mayor's face. "We know about Rosenberg's 'campaign donations.' Admit it, Delgado! You were taking bribes!"

Delgado froze. "I'm sorry... what?"

"You heard me!" Teeny said. "Right? Did you hear me?"

"Yes. I... I think I did." Mayor Delgado looked around. The parking lot was still empty, and Deb and Sandra were long gone.

Linda took a deep breath. "Let's talk in my office."

30

NECTARINE DREAM

$\mathcal{I}$ had been in the mayor's office before. I remembered a modest space with lots of diplomas on the walls. But the place had changed since I'd seen it last, and not in a good way. There were at least thirty degrees on the walls, with no more than half an inch between each. *If these walls could talk*, I thought, *they'd be insufferably stuck-up.* Like a Harvard graduate on steroids.

Mayor Delgado poured us each a glass of water and sat us in leather chairs opposite her desk.

Then she took a seat in her own chair and exhaled. "OK. Tell me what you think you know."

"It might be better if you told us what was going on first," Miss May said. "So we could corroborate the details."

The mayor shook her head. "I'm not doing this on your terms, May. You tell me what you know or you leave."

Miss May stammered. "OK. Uh. Then I guess I'll talk."

Over the next few minutes, Miss May shared every ounce of intel with the mayor. I expected the mayor to look nervous as Miss May spoke, but the more Miss May said, the more relaxed the mayor's posture and face became. Even as

Miss May detailed our knowledge of Rosenberg's bribes, the mayor seemed at ease.

When Miss May stopped talking, the mayor laid her hands flat on the table and nodded. "Everything you just said is true."

Miss May choked on a sip of water. "I'm sorry. What?"

"I knew it!" Teeny pumped her fist. "She's a crook! May, you hold her down. Chelsea, you karate chop her! That's not from *North Port Diaries*, I'm just winging it now!"

"No one needs to karate chop me," the mayor said. "You need to let me explain."

Miss May placed a calming hand on Teeny's arm. "It's OK, Teeny." My aunt turned back to the mayor. "Go ahead."

"OK," Mayor Delgado began. "This all started about a year ago when I was shopping for nectarines at the organic market. Thinking back now, that was a mistake. The organic market charges too much for nectarines. I should have gone to the local grocery."

"How is this related?" Teeny asked. "You were spending the bribe money on organic nectarines?"

"No," the mayor said. "The fruit shopping came before the bribing."

Teeny glared. "That's what they all say. You rotten, no-good, corruptible—"

"Teeny!" Miss May said. "Let her talk."

Teeny settled down and the mayor continued. "OK," Delgado said. "The market didn't have nectarines, so I bought peaches."

Teeny scoffed. "This is absurd. She's buying time."

"I'm sure that's not true, Teeny." Miss May narrowed her eyes. "But I would like to know how this relates to the bribes."

"Me too," I said. "Did Rosenberg know you'd accept

bribes because you so willingly abandoned nectarines for peaches?"

The mayor sighed. "Forget the fruit! I was shopping in the store. About a year ago. When two men in black suits approached me. The men claimed they were from the FBI. They asked me to get into an unmarked car but I refused. So we went to the donut shop next door instead."

"Oh," Miss May said "So you must have been at the organic market down-county. I thought you were at the one near here."

"Down-county, yes," Linda said. "I try to shop local, but I was in the area for another errand, so."

"Good to know," Miss May said.

Teeny threw up her hands. "Why is that good to know? She has said nothing real yet. FBI agents in an organic market? That's nuts!"

"Please let me finish," the mayor said.

"Continue," Miss May said. "And include any details you'd like. You never know what might be a clue."

Miss May shot a look at Teeny, and the mayor kept talking.

"OK. So we went to the donut shop. There, the agents showed me their identification. Then they told me they suspected Hank Rosenberg of bribing community officials to grease the wheels on his big construction projects."

I gasped.

"Exactly," the mayor said. "The feds hadn't caught Rosenberg in the act. But they knew he was eyeing Pine Grove as his next development site. And they told me Rosenberg would likely offer me a bribe in the next few days. They wanted me to accept the money so I could earn Rosenberg's trust."

"Likely story," Teeny said. "I've seen one just like it on my show."

"Then you should believe every word she says," I said. "That's where you get all your information."

Teeny narrowed her eyes at the mayor. "That's true. I'll hear her out."

"Anyway," the mayor continued. "I didn't want to get involved but the FBI agents were persistent. They told me it was my civic duty to help catch Rosenberg. And they wanted me to string him along, bribe after bribe, until he offered something big. A million dollars, they said. Apparently the more money someone bribes you with, the more serious the crime."

"So you were part of a sting operation?" Miss May asked.

The mayor nodded. "That's right. And Rosenberg was about to offer me the big bucks… right before his death."

Teeny shook her head. "You're making that up." She turned to Miss May. "You're not buying this curdled milk are you?"

"I'm not sure." Miss May looked over at the mayor. "Secret agents. Bribery. It seems far-fetched for Pine Grove."

"Massive Mart seems far-fetched for Pine Grove," said Delgado. "Bribery, corruption… that's the stuff that's behind these enormous stores."

"So you never really supported the project?" I asked.

The mayor shook her head. "No. But I had to let the process keep going until Rosenberg came through with the mega-bribe. I told the FBI agents, the day the demolition was supposed begin I planned to shut it all down."

Miss May shook her head. "But that makes no sense. Rosenberg is dead and his parent company is still going forward with the demolition. They parked the wrecking ball on Main Street today."

"That's the problem," the mayor said. "Rosenberg was getting played by this company. They invested a bunch of money but had some shady intentions. I don't know all the details. But supposedly the parent company is a separate legal entity. The papers I signed that gave approval for the Massive Mart are binding, even though I only signed them at the insistence of the FBI. So this parent company claims it had no awareness of the bribes and says there's nothing I can do to stop construction."

"Why was Rosenberg still bribing you if you had already signed binding papers?" Miss May asked.

"He had moved on to a mega mall, and I was pretending to support that too."

Miss May shook her head. "My goodness. So what now? This parent company says we're stuck with the Massive Mart and you're accepting that?"

"Of course not," the mayor said. "Why do you think I'm here so early? I'm trying to find a solution. Those FBI agents are the first on my call sheet this morning."

"I don't buy it," Teeny said. "You're corrupt! You'd do anything in the name of progress and power! This is just like those stoplights all over again."

"Those stoplights were for safety," the mayor said. "But I understand your doubts. Maybe this will change your mind."

Delgado stood up from her desk, climbed onto her chair, and glided her hand along the top of the curtain valance. Seconds later, she climbed back down, holding two tiny electronic devices in her hand.

She put the devices down on the desk and Teeny, Miss May and I gathered to get a closer look. Teeny put on her glasses and squinted to see the little devices. Neither was bigger than a fingernail and each featured a tiny blinking red light.

"What are these?" Miss May asked.

"These are listening devices. The FBI installed them and used them to observe my meetings with Rosenberg."

The mayor walked around the room and retrieved a dozen other listening devices from other hiding places. Under the table. Inside a lamp. Behind one of her eighteen million diplomas.

Teeny remained suspicious. "These devices prove nothing. Maybe you had them installed because you were bribing people or extorting them and you wanted collateral. Anybody can buy this stuff. My nephew bought spy equipment on eBay and used it to catch his mechanic taking a nap in his car."

Mayor Delgado shook her head. "Fine. You want real proof? Indisputable evidence?"

Miss May, Teeny, and I exchanged looks. *Yeah. We did.*

Linda crossed to her desk and dialed a number on her speakerphone. The phone rang a few times. Then a robotic voice crackled over the line.

"Please enter verification code. Please enter verification code."

Linda entered what had to be at least 50 numbers into her phone, by heart. She shot us a satisfied glanced as she entered the last number. Finally, the phone rang again and a gruff, male voice answered.

"This is Agent Gomez," said the man over the phone.

"Agent Gomez," the mayor said, "this is Linda Delgado. In Pine Grove."

"Again? I told you. We're working on it. I'm running it up the chain."

"My constituents do not want to see that Massive Mart constructed. And neither do I," the mayor said.

"Yeah. You mentioned," said Agent Gomez. "I'm on it. But can we talk later? I'm undercover in the sewer and the more I talk the more the odor seeps into my mouth."

"Keep me informed." Linda hung up.

Miss May, Teeny and I sat there. Flabbergasted.

Then mayor crossed to her door and opened it. "Don't forget to vote for me in next year's election."

31

SUDDENLY NO SUSAN

*T*eeny, Miss May and I climbed into the van in stunned silence. A massive scandal had hit our small-town mayor square in the chest. And although Delgado's job description included little more than potholes and traffic lights, this bribery scandal had embroiled her in the most drama Pine Grove had seen since Prohibition.

I felt a shockwave of sympathy for Mayor Delgado. She hadn't shown it, but the past few months must have stressed the mayor beyond belief.

FBI agents. Secret bribes. Toss in a couple dead bodies? It surprised me the mayor hadn't ballooned to 900 pounds from stress eating potato chips and swallowing gum balls whole.

That's normal stress-eating, right?

I turned to Miss May. "What do we do now?"

Miss May shrugged. "First we decide if we believe what we've witnessed."

"It seemed credible," I said.

Teeny stuck her head up from the backseat. "I agree. That thing with the phone. And the hidden recording devices. She didn't know we were planning to show up there. I don't think she could have prepared all that proof just for our benefit."

"I'm not suggesting the mayor prepared anything for us," Miss May said. "But what if she didn't tell us the whole truth? What if her deal with Rosenberg went bad and she took matters into her own hands?"

I shook my head. "That's not the impression I got."

"I know," Miss May said. "Me neither."

"You're just being friends with the devil?" Teeny asked.

"I'm playing devil's advocate, yes," Miss May said. "But if we don't think the mayor did it, we only have one suspect remaining."

Teeny and I exchanged glances.

"Susan?" I asked.

Miss May nodded.

"I guess that's true," I said. "If the mayor didn't commit these murders, Susan makes the most sense."

"I don't know," Teeny said. "May. Remember the cookie party Susan had last year? Her Peanut Butter Thumbprints were so delicious."

"So?"

"So do you really think the woman who baked those treats could have killed her husband in cold mud?"

"Cold blood," I muttered.

"Whatever!" Teeny glared. "You get what I mean."

"Cold mud doesn't make any sense," I protested.

"Susan's cookies were delicious," Miss May said. "But I don't think that means she's innocent."

"So let's go with the theory that Susan killed Rosenberg," I said. "But then who killed Wallace?"

"Hold on a second," Miss May said. "What if Wallace

killed Rosenberg over the apartment thing? And then Susan killed Wallace to avenge her Rosenberg's death?"

"I doubt she'd care enough," Teeny said. "I mean, the woman wanted a divorce."

"That doesn't mean she didn't love him," I said.

Miss May looked over at me. "You speak from experience?"

"Kind of. I mean... Mike is a scum bucket who left me at the altar. But his death would devastate me. I guess human emotions are complicated like that."

"That is complicated," Teeny said. "But also you're crazy."

Miss May turned back to Teeny. "Crazier than the woman with separate rooms for everything? And aren't those cookies maybe a little too perfect?"

"No cookie is too perfect for me," Teeny said. "But I do think Susan might have done the deed. It's like they always say, 'You can take the pickle out of the juice, but you can't take the juice out of the pickle if your dad already cleaned the jar."

"No one says that," I said. "I'm sorry, I'm not trying to be a know-it-all. But no one says that about pickles."

"Why are you always picking on me?" Teeny huffed.

"Will you two quit it?" Miss May said. "It's seeming more and more likely that Susan is a killer. And if we keep chatting in this parking lot she could get away. Or strike again."

"Way to kill the mood," I said.

"Now is not the time for murder puns, Chelsea," Miss May said.

I threw up my hands. "Then when is!?"

"Fine," Miss May said. "That was a fine time for a pun. But if Susan's the killer, we need to get over there. Fast."

I buckled up and Miss May screeched out of the parking lot. Off to find another killer in Pine Grove.

When we arrived at the Rosenberg's big creepy castle, no one was home. I hate to admit it, but the empty driveway relieved me. *Sometimes when you're about to confront a killer, it's nice to take a raincheck. What can I say?*

"No one's home," I said. "Oh well. Let's go get lunch. Suddenly I'm in the mood for a pickle sandwich."

"That's disgusting," Miss May said. "And a bad idea."

"Nu-uh!" I said. "It's a delicious combination, you just haven't tried it."

"I'm not talking about the pickles," Miss May said. "I don't think we should take off just because Susan isn't home. I think we should look for clues."

Teeny crossed her fingers and closed her eyes. "Please say we can sneak inside. Please say we can sneak inside. Please say we can sneak inside."

Miss May grinned. "I think maybe we should sneak inside."

Ugh.

Moments later, I stepped into the Rosenberg's backyard and my eyes widened. The place felt like a cross between a retirement community and a luxury oasis. Lush rose bushes lined a stately stone wall around the back of the yard. A beautiful in-ground pool beckoned from an inset stone patio. And a pristine bocce ball court had been built beside the garden.

I loved everything about the place. Miss May did not. "This is a bizarre backyard," she said. "Too pristine. Too tidy."

"And who has a bocce ball court in suburban New York?" Teeny said. "So weird."

"That's not even the weirdest part of this place," Miss May said. "Wait until you see inside."

Teeny's smiled. "Oh yeah! The creepy separate rooms. I can't wait."

I turned toward Teeny. "You didn't see the inside of the house at the cookie parties?"

Teeny shook her head. "Susan hosted those at her country club, remember?"

"I hope she's innocent," I said. "I kind of want to go next year."

Teeny's eyes lit up. "Oh! We could try a copycat recipe. Head back to the bakeshop and whip up a batch."

"No one is going back to the bakeshop." Miss May looked up at the massive home. "We need to find a way inside."

Teeny waved Miss May off. "That'll be easy. Remember how nimble I am? I'll hop into the window like a little kangaroo." Teeny hopped around on one foot.

"I don't think any hopping will be necessary." I gestured toward the house. "That sliding door is open a crack."

"Phooey!" Teeny said. "But convenient."

Miss May and I laughed and headed toward the sliding door. But before we got there a teenage girl emerged from the house, holding a chubby little cat.

The cat looked just like the girl. Squinty eyes, grumpy face, and a layer of baby pudge. They were both cute but a little scary. *Like I wasn't sure if they were planning to hug me or bite me.*

The girl narrowed her eyes when she saw us, but Miss May jumped in with a big smile before the girl spoke. "Hi there! How are you doing today?"

The girl looked confused. It didn't seem possible, but she narrowed her eyes even further. And she spoke in a nasally voice that surprised me. "Why are you smiling at me? You have perfect teeth. It's making me uncomfortable."

"Thank you so much for noticing. I had braces in my thirties, believe it or not. It wasn't easy, but the results have paid off."

The girl held her cat close. "If you're selling something I'm not buying."

Miss May chuckled. "We're not selling anything. We're the interior designers. Your... mom? Susan. She hired us."

"You mean my aunt. My aunt Susan."

Miss May nodded. "That's right. And what did you say your name was?"

"Gwyneth."

"Gwyneth. Beautiful name. Anyway, Gwyneth. We're here to help your aunt redecorate. But why am I talking? My associate Chelsea is the lead designer on our team."

I croaked. "Yup. That's me."

A confused look passed over Gwyneth's face. "I don't get it. Are you from the same company as the designers who were here yesterday?"

"Yup!" Miss May didn't miss a milli-step. "Those were our junior associates. Now Chelsea is here to make the final decisions. Do a few sketches. You know, interior design stuff. That is such a cute cat. What's its name?"

"Oh," Gwyneth said. "This is my noble little mister. His name is Alan Greenspan. I got him last year when we were learning about the Federal Reserve. He's tremendous. Just like the real Alan Greenspan."

"Alan Greenspan, eh?" Teeny stepped forward. "He's not single by any chance, is he?"

Gwyneth wrinkled her nose. "I don't know. Do cats date?"

Teeny shrugged. "In this town they do. And I think I might know the perfect match."

"But we're not here to bring cats together as life mates and partners," Miss May said, steering the conversation back toward our mission. "So we'll just head inside."

Miss May stepped past Gwyneth and entered the Rosenberg house. "You have a nice day now."

Teeny and I followed Miss May inside.

I breathed a sigh of relief as soon as Gwyneth was in our rearview. "Wow. That was a close one. That girl—"

"OK. So do you want to tell me what you're thinking for the design? My aunt wants me to pass on pertinent information."

We turned around. There was Gwyneth. And there was Alan Greenspan. Both staring at us with their intense, judgmental eyes.

And thus began the most nerve-racking interior design consultation of my career.

32

DESIGN TO DIE FOR

Teenage girls by reputation are flighty and unfocused. Much to my dismay, Gwyneth was neither. She had refined taste, high expectations, and an attitude to match.

As soon as Gwyneth had closed the screen door, she gestured to the drawing room we had entered. "Let's start here. My aunt expects something exquisite at every turn. I want to hear your pitch on what you would do to make this room, and I'm quoting Aunty here, 'divine.'"

I looked around and it surprised me to see the room was drab. There was a floral couch along one wall. Dentist-office-art decorated another wall. A coffee table lingered off to the side like a weirdo at a cocktail party. *OK. Like me at a cocktail party.*

"OK," I said. "I think there's a lot of potential in this room."

"Potential is meaningless without a visionary to bring it to fruition," Gwyneth said. "I believe Alan Greenspan said that once."

Alan the cat meowed. "Not you, kitty. Alan Greenspan the human man."

Miss May nodded. "I agree, Gwyneth. You're smart. You must be an advanced student at your school."

"Please don't butter me up." Gwyneth scratched Alan Greenspan behind his ear. "This interior design job will make your company's fiduciary quarter sing like a mocking-bird in a Las Vegas casino. You want the job, you need to earn it. And let me tell you, those fools you sent yesterday did not impress me."

"I understand." Miss May turned to Teeny. "How about you and I look around the rest of the house while Chelsea and Gwyneth review the plan for this room?"

Teeny smiled. "Sounds like a great idea. We'll see if we can find some clues."

Gwyneth narrowed her eyes further yet. *How could she see like that?*

"Clues? What are you talking about?"

Teeny gulped and made a series of noises that weren't quite words. "Fllllffff. Haaaaannn. Owwwphhh. Shhhhh."

Miss May stepped in. "'Clue' is the word we use for inspiration. We try to find clues everywhere we go. Because each room is a mystery waiting to be solved."

The girl nodded. "Interesting. You've impressed me. Go. Find your clues."

Miss May and Teeny exited and Gwyneth turned to me. "OK. Let's get down and dirty, flirty thirty. And don't forget: the more specifics you provide, the better."

"I'm not thirty yet," I said.

"Figure of speech. Talk."

I nodded. Wiped the sweat from my forehead and wished I could also wipe it off of the small of my back. But something told me I needed to maintain more decorum than that in Gwyneth's company.

"Um... OK. Let's start by discussing windows. Now this room has plenty of light and those sliding glass doors are incredible. And I think we can use the abundance of glass as a pivotal element in our design."

The girl shook her head. "Basic. Boring. Do you want this job or do you want to go on unemployment?"

"Uh, that's not how unemployment works," I said. Gwyneth glared. "But yes. Sorry. I want the job."

Weird. The job wasn't real, but I really wanted it. Perhaps I missed the competitive spirit of pitching prospective clients, I thought. Since I had left the city, I had only decorated for events at the orchard and in our event barn. But Gwyneth activated a dormant part of my personality and transformed me into a superhero, like an interior design version of Jason Bourne. *Maybe I could seek more jobs on my own,* I thought. After we solved the murders.

Gwyneth snapped three times fast. "Hey. Stop daydreaming. You're on the clock, lady. I want to hear something good. Original."

I took a deep breath and glanced around the room once more. It wouldn't have been difficult to suggest switching out the furniture for a few mid-century modern pieces, painting the walls an elegant gray and adding a pop of color. Those ideas were tried and true. But somehow I couldn't make myself suggest normal design. Instead, *you guessed it*, I got nervous and babbled.

"First thing you need to do is demolish that far wall," I said. *Wait, what?! Why did I say that?*

The girl looked over at the wall. "I'm listening."

"I'm assuming there's a dining room on the other side?" I asked.

The girl nodded.

No turning back now.

"Dining rooms are over. Antiquated. No one eats in dining rooms anymore. Life is casual in the modern era, and so is eating. Light, hip, fun. Restaurants barely even have tables anymore."

I knew what I was saying was ridiculous but Gwyneth seemed intrigued. I barreled ahead.

"So I think this room should be an anti-dining room. No tables, no chairs. Just... hammocks."

"Hammocks?"

"Several hammocks," I said. "Hanging from the ceiling. And potted plants, too. Hundreds. I want people to look up and see a labyrinth of plants and hammocks dangling from above. Think modern jungle with a romantic twist."

I knew my ideas were absurd. And the phrase 'modern jungle with a romantic twist' would disgust my colleagues from design school.

Fortunately my audience was a 15-year-old girl with a cat named Alan Greenspan. She was eating it up with a knife and fork, typing notes into her smart phone. My radical suggestions were edgy, and that seemed to be what Gwyneth wanted.

"Now this is refreshing," Gwyneth said. "Keep going. Keep going."

I stammered. *How do you follow potted plants and hammocks?* Lucky for me, Miss May burst back into the room at that exact moment.

"Chelsea! We've got to go."

"What? Why?" Gwyneth asked. "We were just getting started."

"We had a design emergency," Miss May said.

Gwyneth crossed her arms. *Guess her eyes couldn't get any more narrow.* "What kind of design emergency?"

Teeny grabbed her head in a panic. "My armoire exploded!"

"Oh my goodness," Gwyneth leaned forward. "Really? You must have left something plugged in. I hope you have good insurance."

"Insurance? What insurance? For an armoire? No, I'm screwed. I'm never gonna see a dime of that armoire money," Teeny said. "OK bye!"

Teeny and Miss May hurried away. I muttered a good-bye and followed. Teeny poked her head back in before we left. "I'll be in touch about finding love for Alan Greenspan."

Miss May and Teeny exploded with conversation as soon as we got back into the van.

"Oh my goodness I can't believe it!" Teeny said.

"Crazy!" Miss May agreed.

"We should have thought of this sooner," Teeny said. "And it was all just sitting right there!"

"Well we're here now. So let's talk next steps."

"Slow down!" I said. "What's going on? Tell me what happened!"

Miss May shoved an enormous photo album into my lap. Scrawled handwriting labeled the album: "Rosenberg Family Photos: 1950 to 1965."

I narrowed my eyes. "You two are super-excited about a stolen photo album from the 50's?"

Teeny's eyes lit up. "Open it."

I opened the photo album. Black-and-white photographs of the Rosenbergs populated the pages.

Wedding photos. Images of children playing sports. Photographs of kids around a fireplace.

"I don't get it," I said. "This looks like the album from the briefcase. But what's the significance?"

"Turn the page," Miss May said.

I did as Miss May instructed.

And that's when I noticed the clue that would break our case wide open.

33

OH BROTHER

*A*s I squinted at the photo in front of me, I saw that one child gathered around the fireplace had no face. *He had a face in real life*, I assumed. But his head had been cut out of the picture with what appeared to be very dull scissors.

I flipped the page.

Again, the faceless child stared back at me. *Or didn't stare, I guess.*

Page after page contained the same. A mother. A father. And two boys, the older of whom had had his face removed in every picture.

After thumbing through the entire album, I realized my arms were covered in goosebumps. I slammed the album shut and turned to my aunt.

"What does this mean?" I asked. "Do you think Hank is the boy with no face?"

Miss May shook her head. "We think Hank is the one who cut the brother out of the photos."

Teeny leaned forward. "And then Hank cut that brother out of his life. Completely."

Thunk. Teeny dropped another photo album on my lap.

"Rosenberg family photos: 1990 through 2015."

I looked over at Miss May. She nodded. "Open it."

I opened the photo album and saw grown-man Hank with his elderly parents. But there was no more faceless brother, only a conspicuous absence.

There was the family of three at the parents' 50th wedding anniversary. There they were again on vacation in Hawaii. And there the trio was again, smiling at the grand opening of one of Hank's Massive Marts.

"Maybe the brother died before he reached adulthood," I said.

Miss May shook her head. "I don't think so. Who would scratch out the face of a dead little boy?"

I felt a stab of vicarious regret in my stomach. I'd lost my parents when I was so young. I would have given anything to spend just an hour more with them.

Just to say hello to them one more time, or to hear their voices. Or the sound of their laughter. To eat a meal with them or watch a silly TV show. *How easy it could be to take those tiny moments for granted with the people you love.* And how funny that those are the things you miss most when they're gone. The boring, the mundane, the every day.

I turned to the back of the album and saw a few pamphlets from the funerals of both of Hank's parents. They had died close together, three years prior. Hank had most likely paid for the funerals. I wondered if the faceless child had attended his mother's or father's funeral. Then I realized I was getting ahead of myself.

I turned to Miss May. "So what's the theory here? This boy with no face... Do we think that's Hank's brother? Did Hank... murder him?"

Teeny chuckled. "You sound like me. That's an episode of the *North Port Diaries*."

"Then what do we think happened?" I asked.

"We're not sure," Miss May said. "But from where I'm sitting, it looks like the Rosenberg family had a black sheep. And Hank may have exiled his brother. All Hank's success, his money... the brother had no part in it."

I gulped. "You think the black sheep might have gone baaaad and gotten revenge?"

"Insensitive time for a sheep pun, but yes," Miss May said. "It's also possible that this estranged sibling fell on hard times. Lost a few marbles. Sound like anyone we know?"

"Wallace the Traveler," I said. "You think Wallace was the faceless boy. He killed Hank. Then... he threw himself off that hill?"

"It's possible," Miss May said. "But if Wallace wasn't the missing Rosenberg, that means the killer is still out there. And we have a good idea where he might show up next."

"How? Where?" I asked.

Miss May handed me a piece of paper with an address and time scrawled on it. "That's an address for a lawyer in Scarsdale who specializes in wills and estates."

"So..." I wasn't connecting the dots.

Miss May looked me square in the eye. "She's reading Rosenberg's will in twenty minutes."

34

THE FACELESS AND THE FURIOUS

*T*he shopping mall we pulled into that afternoon was the fanciest I had ever seen. There was a store that sold high end men's clothing. A few doors down was a shop that seem to only sell $40 soaps. And next to the swanky soap store were the offices of "Stephanie Connors, LLP. Trusts and Estates Specialist."

According to the note that Miss May had snagged from the Rosenberg house, the reading of the will began at 3 PM sharp. We pulled into the parking lot about ten minutes past three and parked in a corner space under a tree.

"OK," Miss May said. "I think we should go inside."

I wrinkled my nose. "No sneaking? No stakeout? You just want to walk right in? The killer might be in there."

"I agree with Chelsea," Teeny said. "And what will you say when you come face-to-face with Susan? You're the most famous sleuth in town."

"I'm one of two-and-a-half sleuths in town," Miss May said.

"Why can't I be a full sleuth?" Teeny asked. "Is it because I'm short? That's discrimination."

"No," Miss May said. "You just aren't always as involved in the cases. You're part time in the sleuthing game."

Teeny glared. Miss May chuckled. "OK, fine. We're three sleuths."

Teeny did her little golf claps and smiled. "Good. I do at least a third of the mystery-solving."

"Anyway," Miss May said. "I don't think Susan or the estranged brother would dare to confront or hurt any of us in a lawyer's office in the middle of a shopping center like this. Even if one of them is the killer that M.O. doesn't fit either of the previous two killings. One in an abandoned trailer late at night. The other all the way up in the woods."

I nodded. "Fine. But we at least need a plan before we go in there. What are we going to say when they see us?"

Miss May didn't miss a beat. "My great great uncle died. We need to talk to the lawyer. He had lots of money from crayon manufacturing in the early 20th century."

"Did they even manufacture crayons back then?" I asked.

Teeny leaned forward. "In fact they did. And right in this area, too. Crayon manufacturing began in Peekskill right around—"

"Let's skip the history lesson," Miss May said. "Although I appreciate you defending the historical accuracy of my fictional dead uncle's fortune."

I nodded. "OK. That's not quite a foolproof plan, but I guess we could try it. If you're sure."

Miss May smiled. "Sometimes you just need to lean in, Chelsea."

I exhaled. "Whatever you say, Master Skinner."

Miss May opened her door and climbed out. "Let's go."

Teeny didn't budge. "Hold on a second."

Miss May turned back.

Teeny wrung her hands. "I've never been with the two of you for a big bust," she said. "Do you think... Is that what this is? Are we busting the bad guy?"

I hadn't considered it, but Teeny was right. She had always been busy in the restaurant or otherwise indisposed when we apprehended suspects. And she'd always been furious to miss out on the fun of the final showdown. But now that it was go-time, Teeny seemed intimidated.

Miss May shrugged. "This could be the last hurrah. But it might be another dead end. No way to know but to find out."

Teeny reached into her purse for her phone. "Maybe we should call the cops."

"You think Sunshine Flanagan will help in a situation like this? She's ignoring these crimes. And this office isn't even in Pine Grove."

Teeny bit her lip. "I guess that's a good point. But I was thinking, maybe instead of going in there... What if I stayed out here with the van? Like a getaway driver. If things go sideways in the lawyer's office, you might need a quick escape."

Miss May gave Teeny a gentle smile. "I think that's a great idea."

Teeny blinked her sparkling blue eyes, like a nervous little puppy about to go outside for the first time. "That doesn't make me a half-sleuth, does it?"

"Nope." Miss May handed Teeny the keys. "Pull around front and wait for us. And keep it running. We might need to get out of here. Fast."

Teeny nodded. "If there's one thing I'm good at, it's driving too fast."

Stephanie Connors had decorated her lobby like a

doctor's waiting room. Fake plants. Cheap, metal chairs. Florescent lights overhead.

A reception area occupied a far corner. No one sat behind the desk, and a small sign read, "back in five minutes."

I gestured at the sign and Miss May nodded. Neither of us were about to wait, even for five minutes. So we circum-navigated the reception area, and set off down a long, dark hall.

A light was on in an office at the end of the hall and loud voices emanated from within. I couldn't quite make out what was being said. But I thought I heard Susan Rosenberg, along with the voice of an angry older man.

Miss May pointed down the hall like a Navy SEAL as if to say, "Follow me back there."

I shot a nervous glance at the "back in five minutes" sign, then followed.

I walked with careful steps, staying silent. And the closer we got, the louder the voices inside the office became.

The woman who was probably Susan screamed. "You are not a part of this family. You never have been. And you don't deserve a cent!"

A calm female voice tried to interject. Most likely Stephanie Connors.

But the voice of the angry man trampled over her. "I'm more a part of this family than you'll ever be, Susan! I don't care what my scumbag brother told you. So don't get it twisted!"

I widened my eyes and looked over at Miss May. "The faceless boy."

Miss May held her fingers to her lips to keep me quiet. She took another quiet step down the hall and I followed.

I listened as we crept. The man's voice sounded familiar

but I couldn't put my finger on it. Then we were just a few feet away. And we got a glimpse inside the office.

A well-dressed female lawyer who I presumed was Stephanie Connors sat behind a large oak desk. Stephanie had long, brown hair and wore expensive, chunky jewelry.

Susan sat across the desk from Stephanie. Next to Susan, pacing the room...was the faceless boy.

Arthur.

Owner and proprietor of the Pine Grove gas station. And the biggest, most vocal opponent of Rosenberg's proposed Massive Mart.

I gasped when I saw Arthur. He looked toward the door with suspicious eyes. "What was that?"

Miss May and I flattened against the wall to conceal ourselves in the shadows.

Arthur peered out into the hallway but looked right past us. *Phewph.*

Stephanie Connors called after him. "Arthur? I'm sure it was nothing. Please. Come back. I think we can reach a resolution here if..."

Arthur reentered the office, closing the door behind him as he went. With that, we could no longer hear the specifics of the conversation. Only muffled voices. Angry shouting. The occasional cold laugh or vulgar expletive.

Miss May looked at me once again with her forefinger pressed to her lips. And I covered my mouth to make sure I wouldn't let out any other audible gasps of shock.

But none of that would matter, anyway.

In less than a minute, the conversation between Arthur and Susan erupted into a knockdown, drag-out screaming match.

Crash!

Something shattered against the wall. I jumped at the sound and covered my mouth with both hands.

Then Arthur screamed. "That was my parents' money. And you're telling me that my rotten, greedy brother didn't leave me a dime? That scoundrel! That dirty, rotten piece of—"

The lawyer muttered something, but Arthur yelled right over her.

"Yeah right! He used every single one of his stinking pennies to destroy my town. My town! Well," Arthur laughed to himself. "Hank's not going ruin anything anymore, I made sure of that. And I won't let anyone else put up that monstrosity in Pine Grove either! I'll do whatever it takes to protect my home!"

The door swung open and Arthur charged into the hall. He exploded past me and Miss May without even noticing us, then he kicked the main door open, and stormed out into the parking lot.

Miss May and I exchanged glances. It couldn't be more clear.

Arthur was the killer.

And from the sound of things, it was up to us to stop him from killing again.

35

FOILED BY FAWNS

*B*y the time Miss May and I got out to the parking lot, Arthur was already zooming away on his motorcycle

Thinking back, Arthur made a cool villain. Riding his vintage motorcycle into the distance, a long red scarf billowing in the wind. But in that moment, I barely noticed. "Let's get him!"

Miss May and I darted to the bus and jumped in.

"Go, go, go!" Miss May said. "Follow that car!"

Screech!

Teeny careened out of the parking lot, a look of sheer panic dancing in her electric blue eyes. "What the heck is going on? Was that Arthur? From town?"

"Yes!" Miss May pointed after the motorcycle. "Stay on him!"

Teeny squealed around a corner. "I hate following people! It's such a hassle! What if he guns it and runs through a yellow? What am I supposed to do then? I did not sign up for this."

"Yes, you did," Miss May said. "You said you wanted to

be the getaway driver."

"There's a big difference between getting away and giving chase, May!"

Arthur turned.

Miss May pointed after him. "He's making a left! He's making a left!"

Teeny made the sharp left after Arthur and we emerged onto a winding country back road.

Arthur looked over his shoulder and sped up.

"I think he knows we're following him," I said. "Also, when did that guy get so cool?"

"He definitely knows we're following him," Miss May said. "We're the only two cars on this road."

Teeny nodded. "And we're driving an enormous yellow vehicle."

"Maybe I should get this old girl painted in camouflage so we don't stick out so bad," Miss May said.

Teeny chuckled. "Big camouflage bus sticks out even more than a yellow one!"

"Watch out!" I pointed up ahead where a family of deer had stopped in the center of the road.

Arthur swerved through the deer like a slalom skier. Once again, so cool. *How did this gas station guy turn into such a big, bad biker?*

"Oh my goodness! The Indian!" I exclaimed.

"I don't think Arthur's Indian, Chels," Teeny said. "Just 'cuz he works in a gas station. Plus they prefer Native American."

"The motorcycle is an Indian," I said. "That's how Arthur got away that night at the trailer. After he killed Hank! Look at him zig and zag through those deer! He must have parked the Indian out back, squeezed out the window and taken off."

"Slow down!" Miss May said. "Deer!"

Teeny slammed on the brakes to avoid hitting the deer. The three of us got whiplash. *But don't worry, the deer were fine.* In fact, they kept snacking on roadside brush for a few seconds. Then they trotted into the brush.

Teeny punched the steering wheel. "We'll never catch him now. Those adorable deer ruined my chase!"

"I've got an idea." Miss May tapped Teeny on the arm. "Turn this thing around."

"That's the wrong direction!" Teeny said.

"Will you just do it, Teeny?"

Teeny grumbled as she did a quick five-and-a-half-point turn. "I do not understand this decision at all."

"I think I know where Arthur is going," Miss May said. "And if I'm right, I also know a shortcut."

I threw up my hands, confused. "How could you know where Arthur is going?"

"Remember what he said in the office? About the Massive Mart? And how he won't let that store ruin our town, no matter what it takes?"

I shrugged. "So you think he's going back to town? To chain himself to the building?"

Miss May shook her head. "I think he's going after Rosenberg's right-hand man."

My eyes widened. "Sudeer? That makes no sense. Sudeer is just following the orders of some big company. Killing him won't solve anything."

"I don't think Arthur's thinking straight right now." Miss May turned to Teeny. "Make your next right."

Teeny nodded and stepped on the gas.

I remembered Sudeer's little babies and sighed. "I hope we get there before it's too late."

36

HASTY HASTINGS HATING

*C*rack. Boom.

I'll never forget the sound of that gunshot echoing across Hastings Pond.

We were less than a mile away when we heard it. But we might as well have been on the other side of the Atlantic. That's how helpless I felt. That gunshot could have meant that we were already too late.

Teeny sped up as soon as the sound echoed. "Was that—"

"A gunshot," Miss May said. "Speed up."

Teeny squealed the bus around a corner. "I'm going as fast as I can!"

Crack. Boom. Another gunshot.

Miss May set her jaw. "Chelsea, call—"

"I'm already on it." I called 911 with hasty, trembling fingers and reported the shots.

Seconds later, Teeny screeched to a stop outside Sudeer's modest home. Arthur had parked his bike out front. The vintage Indian suddenly seemed less like a sweet ride and more like a symbol of doom.

I took a deep breath. "All right. Let's get in there."

I moved to get out of the car but Miss May caught me by the arm. "Slow down. We need a plan."

Crack. Boom.

Another gunshot.

"There's no time for a plan," I said, barely recognizing the sound of my voice. *No time for a plan?! I'm supposed to be the reasonable one!* What was I saying? "Follow me!"

Without thinking, I jumped out of the van and darted around the side of the house.

Once around back, my eyes shot from the window, to the door, to the roof. Searching for a way in the house.

Miss May arrived at my side seconds later. "See a way in?"

I shook my head.

"It's quiet," Miss May said. "Why don't I hear anything?"

That time, it was my turn to hold my fingers to my lips. I gestured at the back window. A bullet hole had pierced the center of the glass.

I stepped toward the broken window and I could hear crashing and grunting from inside.

The sounds of a struggle.

I climbed onto a cinderblock ledge and looked inside. Sudeer and Arthur wrestled on the living room floor. Fighting for their lives.

"They're in there," I whispered.

"Who's winning?" Miss May asked.

I looked back. Arthur had Sudeer pinned to the ground. The gas station owner was older and smaller than Sudeer, but he fought like a killer. And I knew he'd kill again.

"Arthur's winning," I said. "By a lot."

The gun laid on the floor a few feet away. Arthur shoved an elbow into Sudeer's throat and reached for the weapon.

Arthur's fingertips grazed the handle, but the gun was too far away.

I had to do something. So I jumped down from the cinderblock, crossed the lawn and yanked a lawn gnome from the dirt.

"What are you doing? Miss May asked. "Chelsea, wait! Maybe... Maybe I was wrong. The police will be here in a minute. It's not safe in there.."

I looked inside. Arthur was centimeters from curling his fingers around that gun.

"We need to do something. Now."

Miss May sighed. "OK. But be careful. All right?"

I nodded. Then I hoisted the lawn gnome above my head and...

Crash.

I shattered the window with the gnome. Then I used his pointy red hat to clear the shards from the window frame. Wordlessly, Miss May give me a boost and I climbed through the shattered pane.

Arthur and Sudeer looked up from their scuffle as I entered.

Arthur scowled. "Chelsea Thomas. You little idiot. You think you're a detective? Well, this is your last case! And I'll tell you how it ends."

"I already know how it ends," I said. "You go to jail."

"I don't think so." Arthur jumped off Sudeer in a flash and pounced on the gun. Sudeer got to his feet. But then Arthur spun back and pistol whipped him across the jaw with the gun. Sudeer reeled across the room and rattled against a book shelf.

Arthur spun and trained the gun on me. He laughed. "You think you're smart just because you figured out my last name? Because you figured out that my greedy money-pig brother kicked me out of the family? You should be ashamed for snooping like you do! You and your nosy aunt."

Inch by inch, I tried to get closer to Arthur as he spoke. I hoped his monologue would keep him busy and he wouldn't notice me.

"If you stop me from finishing this you're just as bad as Hank and his awful cronies," Arthur said. "You want that? You want to ruin our wonderful town forever? Massive Marts don't belong in Pine Grove. And neither did my brother. That capitalist swine. He turned my parents against me. And I retreated to this tiny little town, alone and angry. I hated it at first. But over the years? I came to love Pine Grove. The simplicity. The slow pace of life. I found a happiness I'd thought impossible after my brother ruined my life. But Hank? He couldn't allow me to be happy. He couldn't leave me alone!"

Arthur gestured to Sudeer. "And this fool is even worse! He lives in this town. Yet he was ready to build that abomination of a store. And for that... He too deserves to die."

"Arthur," I said. "I understand where you're coming from. But—"

Arthur put his finger on the trigger. "Sorry, Chelsea. It's too late to talk your way out of this."

Sudeer cowered in the corner. "Arthur. You don't have to do this."

Arthur's eyes were ablaze with fear and fury. I could tell his animal instincts had taken over. I had no choice but to fight fury with fury.

Good thing my inner animal knew karate.

Thwap!

With one swift spin, I roundhouse kicked the gun out of Arthur's hand.

Arthur stumbled backward, but he soon regained his footing and squared off against me. He smiled.

"You think you're the only person who knows karate? You forget. My horrible little brother was a champion martial artist. And I was at every one of those lessons."

Arthur lunged, but I sidestepped him. But he spun around without missing a step and drilled a karate chop into my arm.

Ouch.

I stumbled back and Arthur advanced.

I blocked the next hit, but Arthur followed with a kick to my jaw and I careened into the wall.

He laughed as I spat blood onto the carpet. But when I looked up, I had a realization.

I had let Arthur back me into a corner. And I had tried to block and defend myself.

But that was all wrong.

I narrowed my eyes. Then I ran toward Arthur, ducked another hit, and delivered a roundhouse kick into his gut.

Arthur fell over a table and I leapt onto him, pinning my forearm against his throat.

"Your must have missed the most important lesson," I said, hearing Master Skinner's voice in my head. "Lean in."

Seconds later, Chief Flanagan stormed through the front door with Wayne. Before I knew it, Flanagan had Arthur cuffed in the back seat of her squad car.

I called out before Flanagan slammed the door, "Arthur!"

He narrowed his eyes at me.

"There's one thing I don't understand... You killed Rosenberg because of your family feud, and because he threatened Pine Grove. You wanted Sudeer dead because he was moving forward with construction. But what did Wallace ever do to you?"

Arthur snarled like the mean alpha coyote in the woods. "Wallace was just another symptom of the decline of our town! He was a lunatic, unhinged and unpredictable. He kept staring at my motorcycle when I drove down Main Street, like he knew some secret about me. So I followed him one day to see if he was onto me. I saw he had stolen Hank's case. And I knew he had to go."

Flanagan slammed Arthur's door closed, climbed into the squad car and drove away.

Wayne joined me as I watched Flanagan pull away and for the first time that day I got a good look at him. He had a perfect 5 o'clock shadow. He stood tall. His muscular chest appeared to be made of steel. But I felt nothing.

"Sounds like things got rough in there. Are you OK?"

I turned to him. "Yeah. I used my karate. I leaned in."

Wayne smiled and nodded. "Amazing. You're amazing. I just wanted to say... thank you. Thanks to you another bad guy is behind bars."

"I didn't work alone, you know."

I looked over at Teeny and Miss May. It had only been a matter of minutes since we'd narrowly escaped death, but they were already laughing about something over by the van. *That's so typical,* I thought. *Best friends forever.*

Shifting my attention back to Wayne, I remembered that I'd also had help from another unidentified source. The knocking cat that had appeared on my windowsill.

Wayne smirked, and I suddenly realized where the cat might have come from...

"Actually," I said. "We may have had help from inside the police force, too."

Wayne raised his eyebrows. "Flanagan?"

I shook my head. "Not Flanagan."

I mimicked the knocking cat motion with my fist. "We had help from a little kitty on my window."

"I'm not sure what you mean," Wayne said. "But uh, hey... How would you like to grab dinner and a movie one night?"

I laughed. "I've heard that's how traditional, small-town people enjoy one another's company in the Western world."

Wayne cocked his head. "What are you talking about?"

I waved him off. "Never mind. Inside joke."

Wayne stood on one leg for a few seconds. "So... is that a yes?"

I grinned. "That's a maybe."

I wasn't sure why I didn't want to commit to a date with Wayne. I enjoyed teasing him. That was part of it. But maybe I also had a deeper motivation.

Wayne and I had shared a big, romantic dance after the last case. But then he'd vanished for months. *Sure.* He had been a witness in a prominent murder case. But was that something I wanted to deal with long-term?

I wasn't sure. And weirdly, that uncertainty gave me confidence.

"OK," Wayne said. "Maybe it is, then."

Wayne walked back toward his car and drove away.

Somehow, even though I'd left things in limbo with Wayne, I felt like I'd leaned in. And I was proud.

Sure, I tripped and fell down on the way back to the van. But for the brief few seconds before that... I felt proud.

37

AFTER PARTY

*A*fter solving the mystery of Hank and Wallace's murders, we planned to host one of our classic wrap parties. And word must have gotten out. Because when we showed up at *Grandma's* the morning after Arthur's arrest, over a hundred people had lined up outside, waiting to celebrate.

Deb sat on a lawn chair, holding Sandra Day O'Connor in her lap. Big Dan and KP talked cars and donuts behind her. Master Skinner led a "waiting in line" meditation behind them.

I also spotted quite a few people I didn't recognize. A cluster of New York City hipsters crowded toward the end of the line, wearing flannel and cross-referencing their smart phones to make sure they had shown up at the right restaurant to meet the right sleuths.

Oddly, *Grandma's* was closed. Teeny was nowhere to be found. The doors were locked. And the lights were off.

Miss May called out to the town lawyer, Tom Gigley, as we walked to the front of the line. "Tom, what's going on here?"

Gigley shrugged. "I don't know. I'm hungry. These hipsters look hungry. I don't know what the heck is up, but Teeny is dropping the ball on this one!"

As if by magic, Teeny emerged from the restaurant with a smile. "Maybe Teeny was waiting to open until her guests of honor arrived."

Miss May and I laughed.

Teeny gestured to the crowd. "Can we get three cheers for our sleuths, people?"

The mob responded with gusto.

"Hip hip hooray!"

"Hip hip hooray!"

"Hip hip hooray!"

The cheers embarrassed me. But Miss May spread her arms wide, soaking in the adoration. Until the fourth cheer started, and she'd had enough.

"OK everyone. Enough cheering. I'm hungry!"

Miss May stepped toward the restaurant, but Teeny blocked her path. "Slow down. The restaurant really is closed today."

Miss May looks confused. "But I thought you were waiting for the guests of honor."

"I just said that to be nice," Teeny said. "But don't worry. I have an even better idea for the big party."

Miss May and I exchanged a look. *What could be better than Teeny's cooking after a long, hard case?*

"I'm listening," Miss May said. "But I was really in the mood for some Bodacious Berry Bake."

Teeny stepped outside, locked the door behind her and addressed the crowd. "OK people. You want to party with the sleuths? Follow me!"

Teeny marched down main street with her hands on her hips. The crowd murmured in confusion. But then people drifted off behind Teeny. And a minute later, it looked like a full-blown parade.

I smiled and jumped in line. But I couldn't help but wonder... *What did Teeny have in store?*

We arrived at *Peter's Land and Sea* about ten minutes later, out of breath from walking up the big hill.

Petey must have heard us coming because he was waiting on the front walk when we approached. He smiled and gave Teeny a big hug.

"Teeny! What's going on here?" Petey asked.

"Don't worry about it, kiddo."

Teeny turned to the crowd, climbed up on a milk crate and addressed the confused and hungry masses. "People of Pine Grove. Fans of the sleuthing team of Chelsea, Teeny and Miss May. Hipsters that came up here to get a look at the local spectacle. You may not know this kid behind me yet. But hear you me, he is one of the best chefs in town. Nay! He is one of the best chefs on the east coast. And this place? *Peter's Land and Sea*? It's the most spectacular restaurant I've ever eaten at. We're going to celebrate the end of the mystery here. And I want you all to come back often. This kid makes a killer bacon, egg and cheese. But lots of his food is fancy, too. I can't even pronounce most of it. So come back for your birthdays, your anniversaries, I'm sure he does funerals too. I want you to promise me you'll be back before we go inside. Do you promise?"

The crowd cheered.

KP called out from the back of the line. "Enough grand-standing! Let us in. We want to eat!"

Petey gave Teeny another hug and thanked her with a tear in his eye. Then he opened the door, and the crowd entered his restaurant.

Ten or fifteen minutes later, the restaurant was abuzz with happy chatter.

Gigley loved the egg sandwiches so much he ate six in a row. KP ate seven to prove he could outdo Gigley. Petey kept the food coming, much to the delight of the crowd.

Everywhere I turned, folks congratulated me and asked me to re-create my fight with Arthur. Miss May had exaggerated my karate skills, so I let people know the fight was no big deal.

But then I scolded myself. I had played a critical role in apprehending Arthur, and my karate skills had been vital. So I decided to demonstrate my sweet moves to anybody who asked.

While I was showing off my roundhouse to the city hipsters, I noticed Teeny and Big Dan talking out of the corner of my eye. Teeny caught me looking and moseyed over to where I was kicking.

"We're just talking donuts, Chelsea, don't be nosy," Teeny said.

"I'm not thinking anything romantic," I said. "I was just wondering... Is he still going to open *Big Dan's Donuts*?"

Teeny was about to answer, but then the mayor climbed onto her table and clinked a glass.

"Hello all. Can I have your attention please?"

KP groaned. "More grandstanding. Great."

But the mayor demanded everyone quiet down, so we did.

"Greetings people of Pine Grove," she said. "I know you're having fun so I'll make this quick. It is my pleasure to announce that a Massive Mart will no longer be built in Pine Grove."

The townspeople clapped and cheered.

But Miss May narrowed her eyes and stepped

forward. "Really?"

The mayor nodded. "The builders don't feel comfortable opening a new store in a town where their employees don't feel safe. And apparently they experienced pressure to abandon the project from a couple federal agencies. So let's celebrate! This is the one good thing these murders have done for Pine Grove."

More cheers erupted. Then Susan Rosenberg entered with Gwyneth and Alan Greenspan the Cat, and Miss May broke off from the crowd to meet them. I followed, egg sandwich in hand.

Miss May approached with a soft smile. "Susan. Gwyneth. How are you two?"

Susan nodded. "Pretty broken up. But we wanted to thank you. However unpopular Hank was, he deserved justice. And you brought him that. I still have one question though... who was it that covered our home in roll after roll of toilet paper?"

"It was a stranger," I said. "An out-of-towner. Someone who was, uh...well, a fan of our sleuthing." I hadn't realized I knew the answer to that question until I'd blurted it out. But it all made sense as soon as I said it.

"Who are you talking about?" Miss May asked, for once not four steps ahead of me.

"You know, the sticky note perp from the *Brown Cow*? She followed us out of the coffee shop that day to where people were protesting. She said a bunch of stuff to me about how sad it was that a Massive Mart might be built in our little town. It had to be her. She covered Rosenberg's house in TP just like she covered Brian's counter in sticky notes."

"Wow. Truly impressive detective work," Susan said, bowing her head slightly.

"I'm glad we could help," Miss May said. I took a satisfied bite of egg sandwich and nodded in agreement.

Susan turned to me. "I also wanted to discuss something else with you, Chelsea."

I looked up from a big bite of egg sandwich. "Me? OK, sure."

"Gwyneth says you have brilliant ideas for my home. I'd like to hire you as my interior designer."

My jaw dropped. "Wow. That sounds amazing. Although, are you married to the ideas I shared with Gwyneth?"

Susan laughed. "The hammocks and hanging plants? I love it. Sounds like just the change I need right now."

Suddenly, Alan Greenspan let out a loud, mournful yowl and scampered to free himself from Gwyneth's arms.

"What is it Alan?" Gwyneth asked in her nasal drawl. "Mr. Greenspan. What's the matter?"

Alan meowed again. Gwyneth set him down on the floor, and he darted across the room...

To where Deb sat with Sandra Day O'Connor.

Sandra leapt from Deb's arms, and the felines ran toward one another like long-lost lovers. The whole scene played out in slow motion, and sparks flew as Alan and Sandra came face to face in the middle of the room.

The cats circled each other. Sandra nudged Alan in the face. Alan withdrew, then returned her nudge. Then the two cats licked one another and purred.

Deb rushed up and burst into tears. "Sandra! You found the one! Finally, you found the one!"

The crowd broke into applause as Sandra and Alan played together. And Teeny elbowed me with a big I-told-ya-so smile on her face. "I knew those kitties would hit it off. Oh! They are going to have the cutest kittens!"

38

A SURPRISE VISITOR

*L*ate that night I strolled down to the barn to chat with See-Saw. Arthur was in jail and I felt good about that. But one or two nagging questions remained, and I figured talking things through with See-Saw might help.

As per usual, See-Saw seemed disinterested for most of the conversation. And she used the bathroom twice while I told her about my showdown with Arthur. But See-Saw's unimpressed nonchalance was a good thing. I didn't want to develop an ego about my sleuthing, and there's nothing like a horse taking a poop in the middle of your story to keep you grounded.

Finally, See-Saw went to sleep, and I figured that was my cue to leave. But when I turned to walk back toward the farmhouse, I ran straight into the chest of a denim-clad man.

That's right. It was Germany Turtle.

"Germany! I'm so sorry. I didn't see you there."

Germany waved me away. "Please. Stop apologizing. I have a bad habit of surprising women in barns. You, specifi-

cally. I've surprised no other women in barns. That would
be creepy. I'm not a barn-stalker. So please, allow me to
rephrase my original statement as... I have a bad habit of
surprising you in barns. This barn, to be exact. And for that,
it is I who shall apologize. I'm sorry for taking you by
surprise."

I laughed. "You have a strange way with words,
Germany."

Germany gave a little bow. I guess he took that as a
compliment? "Words are putty in my hands. Sometimes I
form them into a beautiful bust. Other times, I manage little
more than hideous lump. Alas, such is the struggle for many
artists."

"I see what you mean," I said. "Although I rarely turn my
words into anything other than confusing, awkward
sentences. I guess I talk too much when I'm nervous."

"Are you nervous now?"

"No." I answered quickly.

Germany nodded. "Nor should you be. Despite my
earlier comments about barn-stalking, I am not dangerous. I
am, like my namesake the turtle, a gentle omnivore slow in
races."

We stood there for a few seconds just looking at each
other. I broke the silence. "Did you just come here to tell me
not to be nervous?"

Germany shook his head. "What a terrible waste of time
that would be. Although I can't imagine time could ever be
wasted in your presence."

I blushed. "Then why did you come here?"

Germany smiled and reached into a little leather man-
bag he had slung over his shoulder. He dug in the bag a few
seconds, then pulled out a little maneki-neko. A knocking
cat! Just like the one I had found on my window.

I smiled. "It was you?"

Germany nodded. "It was, my lady. After we first met I squeezed my brain like a sponge, thinking of ways I could impress you. I constructed several pie charts, a bar graph, and a Venn diagram exploring the best route I could take to your heart. Finally, I realized sleuthing is your main passion in life. So... I vowed to help solve your mystery. The mystery of the dead builder and the crazy homeless man, who I later learned was a forest person. May he rest in peace."

I blinked, confused. "So you investigated the crime, left the cat... All that because you liked me?"

I felt a strange warmth in toes. Like suddenly, I was standing on one of those fancy heated tile floors. I couldn't help it. Germany made me feel good.

Germany nodded. "Well said. I did all that because I like you."

"But then... Why didn't you come tell me what you had learned? Why did you set up that elaborate knocking-cat ruse? That wasn't easy to unravel!"

Germany shrugged. "I thought you would like if the clue itself was a mystery. Also, if I'm being honest.... underneath my bravado, charm and charisma, I can be shy. Did the clue prove useful in your investigation?"

I shook my head. "That building in the city was a red herring. The address led us to Wallace, which led us to the briefcase, which helped lead us to the killer. But that was just a convenient byproduct. "

Germany laughed. "I thought that might be the case. But I hope you derived enjoyment from the cat?"

"I did," I said. "So is that it then? You worked up all your confidence just to come here and tell me you were the one who left the cat?"

Germany took a deep breath. Then, as he often did, he

delivered a speech. "Yes, I came here to reveal my identity as the man behind the knocking cat. But I also came to tell you much more than that. I came to tell you I've gained five pounds in muscles since we last spoke. I have a raw beef diet to thank for that. My meals have repulsed me. But I consumed the beef to build muscle. Because you're clearly attracted to men with physical mass. I've also deduced that you're drawn to men in a position of power. Therefore, I have joined the volunteer firefighters here in Pine Grove. Full disclosure: I will not be a firefighter. I'll be working to train the firefighting dogs. Fire hounds. Puppy fire people. But my superiors have assured me I will get to wear a uniform while I work with the hounds. They have also assured me, in writing, the uniform will accentuate the bulkiness of my budding biceps and triceps."

I smiled. "You don't have to get muscles or train fire dogs to impress me, Germany."

"Oh but I do," Germany said. "For one day I shall ask you out. For 'realsies.' That day is not today, for I'm not yet beefy enough to suit you. But that day is coming. And on that day, I intend for you to say yes. For who can deny a date with a man who trains dogs in the skill of saving people from burning buildings?"

With that, Germany bowed. It was a deep, deep bow. And he left without another word.

After Germany exited, See-Saw stirred from her slumber and whinnied.

"I agree," I said. "He's cute."

The End

Dear Reader,

Thank you for reading *Berried Alive*. This was a fun book to write and I hope you liked it!

The next book in this series - *Granny Smith is Dead* - continues the adventures for Chelsea, Teeny and Miss May.

You're going to love this clean cozy mystery because everyone loves suspenseful cozies with a unique twist. And you won't believe what happens next in Pine Grove.

Search *Granny Smith is Dead* on Amazon to grab your copy today.

Chelsea

Printed in Great Britain
by Amazon

82161594R00161